The Case of the
EXPLODING
LOO

Rachel Hamilton

Rachel Hamilton studied at Oxford and Cambridge and has put her education to good use working in an ad agency, a comprehensive school, a building site and a men's prison. Her interests are books, films, stand-up comedy and cake, and she loves to make people laugh, especially when it's intentional rather than accidental. *The Case of the Exploding Loo* is her first novel, and she is currently working on a second.

www. rachel-hamilton.com

The Case of the
EXPLODING
LOO

RACHEL HAMILTON

SIMON AND SCHUSTER

First published in Great Britain in 2014 by Simon and Schuster UK Ltd
A CBS COMPANY

1 3 5 7 9 10 8 6 4 2

Simon & Schuster UK Ltd
1st Floor, 222 Gray's Inn Road
London
WC1X 8HB

Simon & Schuster Australia, Sydney
Simon & Schuster India, New Delhi

A CIP catalogue record for this book is
available from the British Library.

ISBN 978-1-47112-131-9
EBOOK ISBN 978-1-47112-132-6

Printed and bound by CPI Group (UK) Ltd, Croydon, CR0 4YY

www.simonandschuster.co.uk
www.simonandschuster.com.au

For my family, who put up with a lot

1

WACKY SCIENTIST WIPED OUT BY TOILET BLAST!

I collapse on to the sofa and stare at the newspaper headline.

Wiped out?

WIPED OUT?

Dad hasn't been "wiped out". He's gone missing, that's all. The reporter changed the facts to make a toilet-paper joke. That's just rude.

No wonder everyone thinks something horrible has happened to Dad. The newspapers have been yelling about his disappearance in SHOUTY CAPITAL LETTERS ever since the portaloo exploded forty-eight hours ago.

I screw up the article and throw it across the room. But it's too late; it's already been copied and pasted in my brain. (I'm like Dad's all-in-one printer that way. If I scan something once, it's stored in my memory forever. Dad says it's because I have a photographic memory. Smokin' Joe Slater and the School Toilet Trolls say it's because I'm a mutant freak girl. I prefer Dad's theory.)

Controversial scientist and renowned TV personality, Professor Brian "Big Brain" Hawkins, vanished when an unexplained portaloo explosion shook Lindon's annual Christmas market yesterday afternoon. The top neurologist's smoking shoes were all that remained after the blast rocked the temporary toilet facilities in Lindon town centre . . .

Mum stamps on the novelty Christmas rug, pounding Santa's face underfoot, screaming, "I want to see those shoes NOOOOOW!!!"

Policeman Number PC2746 tries to calm her down. "I'll look into that for you, madam," he says.

But Mum's not listening.

I decide not to listen to him either. Mainly because he's still asking the same dumb questions about what Dad was doing in the toilet in the first place. Um, hello?

I cover my ears against Mum's screams and join my stroppy big sister by the Christmas tree. I'm careful not to stand too close, because Holly's response to Dad's disappearance is to kick everything within reach. That's fine when it's not me she's kicking. But it usually is.

For the moment, she's taking out her fury on the wall beneath the fake-snow-covered bay window. With each kick, she scowls more ferociously at the pack of photographers outside churning up mud in the front garden.

Dad will be mad when he sees the mess they've made of the lines in the lawn. He only mowed it last week. No one else on the street keeps on mowing through Christmas. Dad says it's all about "standards". Holly says it's all about being obsessed with stripy grass.

"We have to do something, Know-All." Holly gives the wall an extra-violent kick. Her voice sounds muffled. My hands are still over my ears.

"The name's *Noelle*." I protest out of habit but I don't hate my nickname. It's definitely better than Mutant Freak Girl. Although Dad says it's good to be a freak when normal people are idiots.

The provocative Professor is best known for his public declaration, "Stupidity is a sickness that should be treated". Only last week, the wacky scientist claimed to have discovered a cure.

The newspapers shouldn't call Dad "wacky". He's not wacky, he's a genius. This is the man who invented "Knife and Fork Fans (For Cooling Hot Food)" and "Gutter-Powered Water Cannons (For Use against Burglars (Who are Scared of Water))".

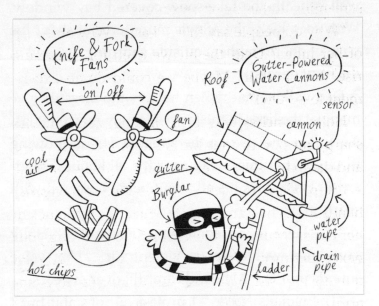

He's been helping me with my inventions too. And he was once voted "Smartest Man on TV" by *TV WOW!* But people will forget all the good stuff because they can't tell the difference between the truth and the news. *I* can. My memory holds a lot of information all at the same time, so I know what's true and what's not true. Even if it's in the newspaper.

Holly puts up a swear finger at the photographers and yanks the curtains shut.

"What?" she says, tugging my hands away from my ears. "Am I supposed to just stand here and let those paparazzi papa-rat-finks take pictures of Mum screaming at the top of her lungs?"

"Why do people say that?" I ask. "Why at the *top* of her lungs? Does the air we need for screaming rise? Like hot air? Maybe we could do an experiment to—? Ow!"

Holly punches my arm, making her knuckles sharp and pointy so it hurts more. Her face is red and damp but she can't be crying. Holly never cries.

"Stop being so . . . so . . . you." Holly shoves her hands in her hair and growls when they get stuck in her curls. "Mum's in bits and you're planning your next experiment? You're as bad as Dad . . ." Her chin quivers and she pulls her right hand free to dead-arm me again. "What's he playing at, Know-All? You're his favourite. He'd have told you if he was going anywhere. Everyone's saying he's d—"

"Disappeared," I interrupt, worried Holly might go for a different "d" word.

Asked about the likelihood of finding Professor Hawkins alive, a spokesman for Lindon Police said: "We haven't ruled out the chance and will continue to work towards that end." However, a source close to the case says, *"The police are assuming the Professor was killed in the explosion. They just want to find out how it happened."*

"Dad's fine," I say. "Just missing. You know what he's like. He's probably working on some big invention and has forgotten the time."

"Forgotten the time? For two whole days?" Holly splutters. "Don't be daft. What about the leather lace-ups they found in the burnt-out portaloo?"

"What about them? They only prove that Dad's *shoes* were in the toilet when it blew up, not that Dad was. The shoes are a red herring."

I know all about red herrings from reading detective stories. Red herrings are fake clues put in place by writers and bad guys to stop you guessing what's really going on. One of the most common is the mysterious death with no identifiable body – or, as I call it, the "Dead Herring".

Dad isn't dead. This is all part of a cunning plan. He's a Dead Herring. Dead Herring Dad.

There must be a hundred reasons why a man might leave his shoes in an exploding toilet and then vanish without a trace. I only need to find one.

2

Three Weeks Later . . .

- Number of theories the police have come up
  with to explain Dad's disappearance = 27
- Number of intelligent theories the police
  have come up with to explain Dad's
  disappearance = 0

Our local police are not displaying the dedication to crime-fighting I've come to expect from watching *CSI: Crime Scene Investigation* on TV. They certainly don't solve as many crimes.

The person who'd be best at figuring out what happened during that toilet explosion is the person who disappeared in the middle of it.

Dad.

Dad is famous for finding solutions – often to

problems the world doesn't even know it has. Not everyone agrees with his ideas, but no one can deny he has them.

What everyone *does* agree with is *TV WOW!*'s declaration that Dad is 'good TV'. Unfortunately, being 'good TV' seems to mainly involve winding up everyone else on the programme until they start yelling at you.

He winds Holly up too.

He doesn't wind me up though – he's too busy helping me. That's why I miss him. With Dad gone, I have to google stuff instead of just asking him for the answer, Mum has to kidnap the milkman whenever a light bulb needs changing, and Holly has no one left to argue with – except me. And I don't like it. It's a painful business arguing with Holly. I've got the bruises to prove it.

So I've decided to help the police by taking over the investigation.

I begin in ICT, on our first day back at school after Christmas, by googling "spontaneous human combustion". That's the police's latest theory:

Spontaneous human combustion describes the burning of a human body without an apparent external source of ignition. There have been about two hundred reported cases worldwide over a period of around three hundred years.

"Two hundred divided by three hundred. Two over three. Two-thirds," I race down the corridor to maths. I always travel around school at speed because a moving target is harder to hit. "How can two-thirds of a person explode per year?" I wonder aloud as I step into the classroom.

"Easier to think of two people exploding every three years," my maths teacher, Ms Grimm, suggests.

Either Ms Grimm has hearing like a super-bat or she's paying far too much attention to what I have to say.

"Sit down. Books out," she barks. "Tell me, Hawkins, have the police made any progress with their investigation into your father's explosion?"

I shake my head, partly to say "no", partly to say "I can't believe you're asking me about this". There are some things you don't want to discuss with your scary maths teacher. But there's no special treatment for kids with missing dads at Butt's Hill Middle School.

Holly and I got the end of last term off, straight after the explosion, but I suspect that was because the head didn't like reporters hanging around the school gates, taking photos of Butt's Hill students smoking, smooching and sneaking out to buy chips.

"No progress at all? What are these policemen doing?" Ms Grimm curls her lip. "You'll need your brain in gear if you want to find out what happened, Hawkins. No more silly questions. Start thinking. You'll never win a Nobel Prize if you can't apply all that information in your head to real-life situations."

Ms Grimm talks about winning prizes a lot. She's anti-stupid, just like Dad.

I search my memory for information on Nobel Prizes:

Every year since 1901 the Nobel Prize has been awarded for achievements in physics, chemistry, physiology or medicine, literature and for peace.

"You don't need to worry," I say as the rest of my class stampede into the cold, grey classroom and dive for the seats near the radiator. "There's no Nobel Prize for maths."

But I think about Ms Grimm's words. What if I have all the information I need to solve Dad's disappearance inside my head and I just need to apply it?

"Seating plan," Ms Grimm bellows at the radiator-huggers.

Everyone scuttles to their proper seat. You don't mess with a woman who looks like she was made from the unwanted parts of several bodies – not all female and possibly not all human.

Everyone at Butt's Hill is scared of Ms Grimm,

including the head, who has given her the biggest office in the building even though she only works Monday mornings and Friday afternoons. No one knows what Ms Grimm does for the rest of the week. Before the explosion I made a pie chart to show the percentage of students supporting each of the most popular theories:

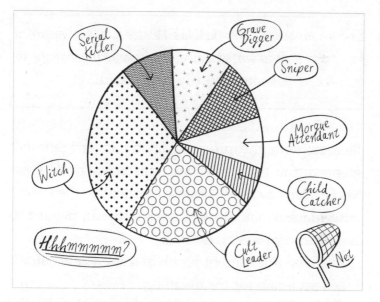

The figures are a bit out of date now as I'm too busy getting my head round Dad's possible spontaneous combustion to think about Ms Grimm's second career. Plus, I'm starting to think we've all got it wrong and she's a private investigator. We've only been back at school for one day and she's already asked me about the police enquiry three times.

I round up my two-thirds of a spontaneously combusting person to make a whole one. But that still means, of approximately fifty-six million people in the world who died last year, only one spontaneously combusted.

My first clue:

CLUE 1
It is statistically unlikely Dad
spontaneously combusted.

Pleased with the progress of my investigation, I glance up at the whiteboard. It's Science Week, so Ms Grimm has asked how we'd calculate the lowest percentage of a mixture of gases in the air needed to create an explosion if ignited.

I've seen this kind of problem somewhere before. I rack my brain for the memory.

Got it! It was on Ms Grimm's whiteboard one morning, after she'd been teaching Gifted and Talented Club the night before.

I put up my hand.

"Hawkins?"

"You could use Chair Mixing," I say. A few

people snigger as Ms Grimm pulls her this-student-is-an-idiot face.

I close my eyes so I can fix the memory of the whiteboard in my mind and read the words written on it:

"Chair Mixing – Divide the fraction of the total volume of each gas by its lower explosive limit to get the partial lower explosive limit of the mixture." I ignore the yawns and vomiting noises from the back of the class. "Then sum all the partial lower explosive limits and take the inverse of that sum to get the net lower explosive limit of the mixture."

"Perfect," Ms Grimm nods. "Le Chatelier's mixing rule."

"Er . . . yes. That." Someone must have rubbed out a few letters on the whiteboard.

"Everyone else get that?" Ms Grimm asks the class.

The vomiting noises stop and someone at the back protests, "We're only Year Eight, Miss."

"So is Hawkins."

"Yeah, but she's a mutant, Miss." Smokin' Joe leans forward, releasing a mouldy stench of stale cigarettes, cat wee and sweaty armpits. "Seriously, Freak Girl, where do you get this stuff? It's creepy."

Creepy? Me? This, from the boy who spends his free time hanging out in the boys' toilets, smoking cigarettes with the Toilet Trolls.

"Ms Grimm wrote it on the..." I tail off as I realise what I'm saying.

CLUE 2

Ms Grimm was calculating how to make things explode a week before Dad's portaloo blew up.

Can it be a coincidence? Is she the one responsible for the exploding loo? Is that why she keeps asking about the police? To find out how close they are to rumbling her?

Maybe the pie chart for Ms Grimm's second career should look more like this:

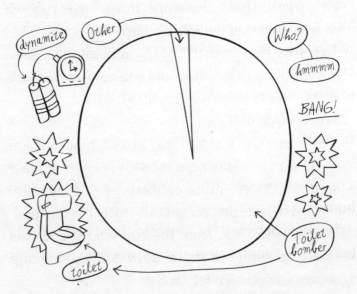

3

Smoking Shoes

I will be redirecting my investigation towards Ms Grimm shortly. But at the moment I'm too busy worrying about Mum. Aunty Vera says Mum's coping badly with Dad's disappearance. Aunty Vera's got it wrong. Mum's not coping badly – she's not coping at all. Now she's stopped screaming and yelling, all she does is lie on the sofa hugging stuffed Santas and staring into space.

The Santa-hugging is particularly disturbing. It's been three weeks since Christmas and Dad would have made us pack the Christmas things away by now, declaring, "A tidy house is a happy house."

He said that a lot. "Maintaining a tidy home is the best way for someone of average intelligence to keep on top of things," he'd tell Mum, patting her on the head. "I know you try your best, dear, but if you kept the laundry room in better order you might remember to iron my boxer shorts."

Post-explosion Mum has given up tidying. And ironing. And ... well ... everything really, except eating curry and lying on the couch.

This is having a worrying side effect. I don't spend a lot of time looking at Mum's bum, but I can't help noticing it's fast approaching the width of the sofa. It has also taken on the sofa's square edges.

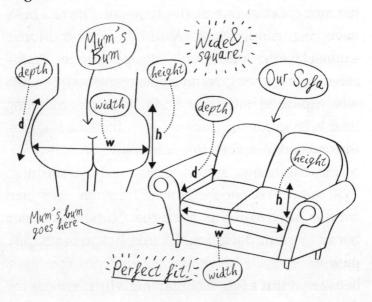

On the upside, this helps Mum slide into place more easily. On the downside, Uncle Max says he's starting to wonder if she ate Dad.

I'm ninety-seven per cent sure he's joking.

Either way, Mum reminds me of the huge inflatable Tyrannosaurus Rex that sat outside the discount shop until it blew away in the storm last month. Like the T-Rex, Mum is big and scary from a distance. Then, when you get closer, she's worse than scary. She's empty, like there's nothing but air and breath where her thoughts should be.

The only time Mum moves these days is to shovel her mouth full of Curry in a Hurry takeaways. These have been turning up every night since the toilet explosion, even though no one orders them. Holly called Curry in a Hurry to let them know and to ask what we owed, but they said the food was a sign of their admiration for Dad's work. Weird, but I guess that means it's okay to eat them. Mum certainly seems to think so.

At first, Holly and I tried to snap Mum out of her curry coma by pulling her to her feet and making her walk around the house, but the more days that pass without Dad and the more curries that pass between Mum's lips, the harder it is to heave her off the couch.

Holly still makes a token effort to get Mum on her feet. I don't. I just sink down on the sofa beside her so we can chat. Admittedly, I do most of the talking, but at least Mum doesn't get up and wander off the minute I mention electromagnetism or scalar waves the way everyone else does.

Besides Dad only lets us watch thirty minutes of TV a day when he's home, so I want to catch as much as I can before he comes back. And he is coming back. I know he is.

Shrek's on today when we get home. I like *Shrek*. So does Holly, but she's been pretending not to since a boy at school told her thirteen-year-olds are too old for animated movies. Ugh, teenagers.

To be fair to *Shrek*, Holly doesn't like anything any more. When Dad was around, she was always yelling how much she hated him for acting like she wasn't good enough. Now he's gone, she's trying to replace him by finding new things to hate.

Before *Shrek* joined her hate list, Holly's favourite scene was the bit when Princess Fiona sings the songbird to death and it explodes, leaving nothing but its tiny yellow feet clinging to the branch. We fast-forward that scene now.

Film and videogame characters are always blowing up and leaving only their shoes/ feet/ hooves behind:

Bond movies:
An evil villain lady called Fatima Blush explodes after being shot with bullet-grenade from Bond's pen. Only her smoking high heels remain.

Kingdom O'Magic game:
Characters find a pair of smouldering boots next to an axe and a tree stump when they enter the Enchanted Forest.

CHARACTERS EXPLODE LEAVING SMOKING SHOES BEHIND

Old Doom videogame:
You can blow up the cyber-demon until only his bloody hooves are left.

Toy Story 2 movie:
In the opening sequence Zurg blasts Buzz into smithereens – leaving only his legs behind (but don't worry. It's just Rex's videogame).

But life is not a film or a videogame, which is a shame because make-believe characters act logically and let you know who the bad guys are.

CLUE 3
Smoking shoes are a movie/video game device, not evidence.

I decide to share my first three clues with the police. Unfortunately, I'm cut off before I get the chance. This has been happening a lot recently.

Holly says it's because I'm a stalker and the police

are fed up with me ringing them five times a day. I prefer to think it's a switchboard problem. So I call again, and again, until the phone is picked up by my favourite policeman, PC Eric. PC Eric sounds older than the other officers and sometimes forgets what he's saying, but he's obviously important because whenever I do get through, I'm usually passed on to him.

PC Eric listens to my theories. "I was suspicious of the shoes at first too. But my colleagues found a report about a group of soldiers killed by anti-tank fire in the 1989 Romanian Revolution, leaving nothing but a pile of ash and several pairs of leather boots."

"Tell your colleagues they shouldn't believe everything they read," I say, "and they *should* investigate Ms Grimm."

"I'll pass that on. I'm sure they'll be grateful."

I suspect PC Eric is not being completely honest. His voice squeaks in the middle, like Uncle Max's when he says Aunty Vera's bum doesn't look big in her flowery dress. I decide to spend some of the £84.73 I've saved for a graphing calculator (with touchscreen) on a pair of leather shoes so I can set them on fire and prove they couldn't withstand an explosion. That should convince the police The Case of the Exploding Loo still requires the attention of their best officers.

We have to find Dad. No one else can help me develop the brain ray we were working on when he vanished. And no one else can out-google Google.

4

Turquoise iPods

When Uncle Max and Aunty Vera pop round to check on Mum, I ask Uncle Max to buy me a pair of men's leather shoes. He looks down his nose at the twenty-pound note I'm offering.

"You won't get a decent brand of shoe for less than a hundred pounds."

"I don't need a decent brand. Dad says people who buy designer labels never have any money."

"Does he?" Uncle "designer brand" Max huffs. "Well, your Uncle Max says people who blurt out every stupid thing that pops into their head never have any friends."

I decide to ask someone else to buy the shoes. Someone who isn't Uncle Max, or Mum, who's still buried beneath Santas, listening to her new turquoise iPod.

This is a clue for three reasons:

1. Mum never joined the Curry in a Hurry
   loyalty scheme.
2. Although Mum gobbles up everything
   Curry in a Hurry delivers, we've still
   never ordered, or paid for, any of it.
3. Turquoise is a weird colour.

The turquoise thing gets even stranger when I spot
the turquoise Kazinsky Electronics van parked on
the opposite side of the road, facing our house.

Clue or coincidence?

"Hideous," Aunty Vera says.

"Mmm," I agree. "Horrible colour."

Aunty Vera stares at me. "What are you talking
about?"

"What are *you* talking about?"

"That painting." Aunty Vera points at the enormous canvas above the fireplace. It arrived the day

Dad vanished with a note saying it was a picture of Dad and should be hung on the living-room wall.

"Why on earth did you keep it?" Aunty Vera asks.

"Dad always keeps the gifts people send him after his TV appearances. He says it's important to respect your fans."

"He had fans?"

I don't like my aunt's sarcastic tone, or her use of the word "had".

"He *has* loads. He calls them the Big Brain Buffs." I don't tell her Holly calls them the Doo-lally Daddicts. "Anyway, this is a portrait of Dad. We can't throw Dad in the bin."

Aunty Vera doesn't look so sure. "Well, I've never seen anything so ugly."

"The note says it's surrealist."

"Mad-as-a-badger-ist, more like."

Aunt Vera reaches for the picture. The minute she lifts it off its hook, Mum starts to scream. She keeps on screaming, not pausing for breath, until Aunty Vera rams it back in place.

As Aunty Vera wipes the sweat from her forehead and Mum relaxes back into the sofa cushions, I try removing the painting again, just for a minute, to see how Mum reacts.

Mum gives the same eardrum-shattering wail. I slam the picture back on the wall.

"Pythagoras!" I shriek and then snap my mouth shut. Holly says my habit of calling out the names of famous scientists and mathematicians at times of stress is one of the reasons I have no friends except Meccano Morris. And he's more a science club partner than a friend.

Aunty Vera hits me with her handbag. "What did you do that for?"

"It was an experiment. I wanted to see what Mum would do."

"Now you know. And know this: any more experiments in my presence and you'll find yourself hanging above the fireplace, alongside that monstrosity."

Aunty Vera can be scary. Holly calls her the Vigil-Aunty, which is a funny nickname unless she hears you say it. Then it's not so funny because she'll hit you with her handbag. A vigilante is someone who takes the law into their own hands to avenge a crime. This makes it a good name for Aunty Vera, because if anyone committed a crime against her she'd vigilante them into small pieces with her Handbag of Mass Destruction.

I gaze up at the picture. "Monstrosity" is a bit harsh, but the surreal Dad picture breaks all the mathematical rules of proportion for drawing a person:

Rules of Proportion —VS— Surreal Dad picture

	Rules of Proportion	Surreal Dad Pic
The Eyes	The distance between the top of the head and the eyes should be half the length of the face.	Surreal Dad's eyes come three-quarters of the way down his face, leaving a very large area for his brain.
The Mouth	The mouth should make up the bottom of a triangle drawn from the centre of the face through either side of the nose.	Surreal Dad's mouth is too small. It's also covered by the pointy finger of the right hand.
The Nose	The nose should fit neatly in the third quarter of the face from the top.	Surreal Dad's nose is too long compared with the other features on the face.

I'm sure it all means something. I just don't know what.

The background of the picture is equally strange. Behind Surreal Dad are two groups of people. The figures on the left have fuzzy features and it's hard to tell where one person ends and another begins. The figures on the right have abnormally large heads and more distinctive features, which show them laughing.

I thought the painting was saying people with big brains are happier until Holly said the big brain people were laughing at the other group. I don't like that idea. It makes the picture feel mean.

If you look closely, you can see a tiny figure half-hidden in the trees between the two groups – a girl with a golden crown perched on her extra-large head. Holly thinks she looks like me. I don't. I don't want to be Princess of Mean People with Big Heads.

Surreal Dad's left hand is holding a piece of paper covered in squares, circles and arrows, with a red cross in the top corner. Above the cross is a word with several letters missing, like a hangman clue: L _ _ _ _ S.

I made a copy of the diagram to carry in my pocket and I've spent all month studying it. But I still don't know what it means. I stare at the painting a lot. So does Mum. Maybe because it means we don't have to look at each other.

I shuffle behind the sofa and make a grab for Mum's Curry in a Hurry earphones. I'm curious to find out what's on the iPod because its arrival has meant the end of my one-sided chats with Mum about electromagnetic waves and I don't like it.

For one mad moment I think I hear Dad's voice. Then Mum screams so loudly I can't hear anything else. I drop the earphones and back away in alarm, covering my ears as I remember what happened to the songbird in *Shrek*.

Aunty Vera shoves the earphones at Mum and tells Uncle Max to hammer another hook above the fireplace. As I flee from the room, I notice Mum's nose is bleeding.

5

Suspects

Mum's nosebleeds haven't stopped and she is steadily being absorbed into the sofa. But I can't let myself be distracted from my investigation any longer, especially now I have a suspect. Ms Grimm ticks two important boxes:

☑ The Means – She knows how to blow things up.

☑ The Opportunity – No one knows what she's up to for most of the week.

However I'm struggling with the most important box of all:

☒ The Motive – Why would Ms Grimm want to blow up a toilet? Or hurt Dad? She's one of the few people who share his extreme beliefs about intelligence.

Dad's views aren't popular, particularly with Smokin' Joe and the Toilet Trolls. I can understand their objection to Dad's declaration that people with low IQs (which stands for "Intelligence Quotient", not "Idiotic Questions" like Holly says) should be banned from voting or having children. But surely there are better ways to protest than setting fire to my textbooks and chucking my shoes into tall trees.

It's a good job Holly likes climbing.

When I told Dad I was having issues at school, he said, "Many have had their greatness made for them by their enemies."

That's a quote from Spanish philosopher, Baltasar Gracian. Easy for Baltasar to say. I bet no one shoved *his* head in the school kitchen wheelie bin, or stuck a Post-it on his back saying "kick me".

"It's your fault for being pathetic," Holly says as she helps me pull wheelie-bin spaghetti out of my hair on the way home from school a week later. "You need to stand up to bullies."

"It's hard to stand up at all after a wedgie."

"Aren't wedgies a boy thing?"

"Smokin' Joe is an equal opportunities bully," I

say, pulling a wheelie-bin carrot from behind my ear. "I don't know what to do. I've tried ignoring him, like Dad suggested, but it's not working."

"Never listen to Dadvice. Dad didn't even follow it himself. Remember when the milkman told him off for calling Mum stupid? No way did those wasps find their way into the empty milk bottles by themselves. Dad wasn't as perfect as you think. Admit it."

"I'm not listening." I cover my ears with the sleeves of my school jumper and cross into our street ahead of her. "La la la."

"Admit it." Holly pushes past me and races for home. "Or when we get in I'll rearrange your books so they're no longer in alphabetical order."

"Okay, I admit it. I ADMIT IT."

I agree, not only because I want to preserve order on my shelves, but also because I remembered the invention Dad asked me to design last year. At the time, I thought the milk-bottle wasp trap was a hypothetical thing. It wasn't.

The Milk-Bottle Wasp Trap!

NO!

cut from plastic bottle

Sugar (Jam)

Milk Bottle

JAM

Protein (canned) tuna

TUNA

Excellent trapper!!

CLUE 6
Dad might not be as relaxed about
his enemies as he pretends.

What if Dad got into an argument with someone more dangerous than the milkman? I should ask the police if they've heard anything. I should also investigate the milkman.

But before that, I need to figure out what that van is doing parked outside our house. What is it with all these turquoise vehicles? This one is similar to the Kazinsky Electronics van that was parked on the opposite side of the road a week ago, but with a rounder bonnet and without the big KE logo on the side.

More worryingly, it's being loaded with boxes through our open front door.

"Mum?" Holly sprints the last few metres. "Mum? Are you okay?"

A quick glance through the out-of-date Christmas lights in the bay window reassures me Mum is still slumped on the sofa, oblivious to van and driver. I'm more concerned about what's in the boxes.

A man in a shiny suit blocks the doorway, showing too many teeth. "Good afternoon, young ladies. I represent your father's life insurance company." Insurance Man wipes a hand on his shiny suit and holds it out towards us. "We're here for 'Removal and Disposal'. It's a standard part of the policy."

Holly ignores the hand. "Why don't we know anything about this?"

"Because you're just girls." Insurance Man reveals yet more teeth as he continues to thrust his hand at us. "We deal with adults and your mother has no problem with me carrying out your father's wishes."

Just girls? Bah!

"Mum has no problem with wearing the same pyjamas, non-stop, for over a month either," I point

34

out. "So she's hardly the best judge of what is and isn't okay. Also, my dad is NOT DEAD!" Why do I have to keep reminding everyone? "So he doesn't need a life insurance policy."

"Nevertheless, I have my instructions." Insurance Man withdraws his hand and puts it in his trouser pocket. "And unless an adult objects, I will be carrying them out. My work colleagues here will deal with your complaints."

He beckons to two enormous men in muscle-vests who are lugging boxes down the stairs. I don't catch their names but they sound something like Ug and Thug.

I look up at Ug and Thug.

Ug and Thug look down at me.

It's hard to put my complaints into words because:

    i. I don't know anything about life insurance.
    ii. Ug and Thug's bulging biceps are VERY LARGE.

Before I can say, "So what exactly is 'Removal and Disposal'?" Insurance Man has filled his turquoise van with boxes and (Th)Ugs and sped away.

"Who was that?" Uncle Max arrives with one of Vigil-Aunty's unidentified-vegetable casseroles.

Holly grabs the casserole and slams it down on the hallway table. "A man who made me want to kick things."

"Ow!" Uncle Max grabs his ankle.

"They were from Dad's insurance company," I explain. "They took a load of stuff for 'Removal and Disposal'. The man said it was part of Dad's life insurance policy."

"'Removal and Disposal'?" Uncle Max barges past me.

He yanks open drawers and cupboards and throws a mantrum in the hallway about some missing Hugo Box cufflinks he'd had his eye on.

"'Removal and Disposal'?" he repeats, stamping his feet like a toddler. "That's not even a thing."

If it's not a thing, it's a clue.

CLUE 7

Someone wants Dad's belongings:
cufflinks, underpants and all.

Clue or not, I wish Fake Insurance Man had left some of Dad's stuff behind. I miss it and I miss him. Dad, I mean, not Fake Insurance Man. I don't miss Fake Insurance Man at all. He slammed doors and smelt of cheese. Dad smells of Imperial Leather soap and breath-mints. But it's not just Dad's cleanliness I miss. I miss the time we spent together discussing the latest discoveries in brain science. And I miss his help with my brain ray invention.

I came up with the brain ray concept last year because I wanted to give people a way to increase their IQ so Dad would like them more. Dad loved the idea and we've been working on it ever since.

Holly thinks it's stupid and says I'll never convince her or Mum to use it.

I've told Holly a thousand times I didn't invent it with Mum in mind. My voice doesn't even squeak, but she still gives me that look that shouts, "Big fat liar".

I notice something while I'm shutting the drawers Uncle Max left open.

"Hey, Holly! Fake Insurance Man took my brain ray sketches. Do you think that's a clue?"

"Definitely." Holly pauses. "A clue he had to grab everything in a hurry."

Hmmph. I write it up anyway.

CLUE 8
Fake Insurance Man took the plans
and sketches for the brain ray
I've been developing with Dad.

6

Theories

I've been considering the most important clues I've
gathered so far and I have reached a conclusion:

(RECAP)
CLUE 1
It is statistically unlikely Dad
spontaneously combusted.

+

(RECAP)
CLUE 3
Smoking shoes are a movie/
videogame device, not evidence.

+

(RECAP)

(RECAP)
CLUE 7
Someone wants Dad's belongings:
cufflinks, underpants and all.

=

THEORY A
SOMEONE HAS KIDNAPPED DAD

When I call the police to share my theory, I get a shock. Dad's disappearance has been officially downgraded to a "cold" case. At first, I think they're referring to the outdoor temperature at the Christmas market, but no. Apparently cases go "cold" when there are no more leads to follow, all suspects have been ruled out and all evidence has been tested.

"But Dad's still missing," I protest to PC Eric. "You're the police. You're supposed to find him."

PC Eric reveals my least favourite clue so far:

CLUE 9
Traces of Dad's blood were found in
burnt-out portaloo along with his shoes.

"Your Dad hasn't been seen for seven weeks," PC Eric says gently. "My fellow officers have drawn the obvious conclusion."

"That conclusion is not obvious to me."

"It's not necessarily what I believe either. But my hands are tied."

I stare at the phone in shocked silence. Who would do that to PC Eric?

"Not literally," he adds quickly. "What I mean is police procedure doesn't always let me follow investigations as I'd like. But there's nothing to stop you making enquiries. Perhaps you'll collect enough evidence to convince us to re-open the case."

"What about my suspect? Did you find out what Ms Grimm does when she's not teaching at Butt's Hill?"

"Yes."

"And . . . ?" This is the answer everyone's been waiting for. "What does she do when she's not teaching at Butt's Hill?"

"She teaches at a school in Lindon."

That's it? That's my answer? When she's not teaching, she's teaching?

Do I need a new suspect? Does the milkman count? How can I get a cold case warmed up again?

"This cold case thing . . ." I say. "Does it mean I can have Dad's shoes from the explosion?"

"I don't see why not. One of our officers will be popping round to explain the change in investigation status to your mother. I'll ask him to bring the shoes."

I pace by the front door, twirling Uncle Max's lighter between my fingers, waiting for the officer to arrive. My plan is to set fire to the shoes the minute the officer hands them over, proving they couldn't survive a blast that combusted an entire person.

But things don't work out the way I planned.

Curry in a Hurry Man arrives just as PC2851 is heading across the front lawn, shoes in hand. Curry in a Hurry Man stumbles over something hidden in the unmown grass and knocks into the back of PC2851, spilling curry all over his police uniform. During the confusion of curry, shouting and Mum having another nosebleed, the shoes vanish.

I search everywhere, thrusting tissues at Mum and keeping a tight grip on PC2851's jacket. He can't leave before my shoe bonfire. He just can't.

But PC2851 uses his police skills to wriggle free and he races down our front path as if it were *his* shoes on fire.

Of course, Dad's shoes reappear within minutes of PC2851's escape. Curry in a Hurry Man returns on his moped and explains that he picked them up by mistake. By mistake? A pair of size tens? How is that possible? I can't even be cross, because Curry in a Hurry Man is so apologetic and so desperate to make it up to me.

"Drink!" Curry in a Hurry Man forces a styrofoam cup into my hand. "I am bringing the world's best hot chocolate just for your good self. This I will be doing every day, thirty minutes after four, to make apologies for my oh-so-clumsy actions."

"Hot chocolate?" I like hot chocolate. "Yum. Thanks. There's no need, but if you insist . . ."

"I am insisting." Curry in a Hurry Man bows and apologises all the way back to his moped. There's a split second, while he's pulling on his helmet, when his expression seems to change into a sneer, but it must be a trick of the light.

Either way, I've missed my chance of convincing the police to warm up the case again.

I sip my hot chocolate. It tastes bitter but I drink it anyway, gagging when I spot a familiar turquoise vehicle on the other side of the road.

CLUE 10

The Kazinsky Electronics van is parked
outside our house almost every day now.

It makes me nervous.

Holly says that's because everything makes me nervous. She might have a point. The van doesn't seem to bother anyone else.

I shuffle upstairs to my room, feeling incredibly tired all of a sudden. I fall asleep hugging Dad's shoes. Other people have fluffy teddies to cuddle. I have a pair of slightly scorched leather lace-ups. When I wake up an hour later, the thought of burning them makes me shudder.

I don't know what happened while I was asleep. I never get attached to anything that doesn't have internet access, but for the rest of the day I find my hands automatically reaching for the shoes and stroking them.

7

The Importance of Names

Holly decides that if the police are no longer investigating Dad's disappearance then we need to find our own witnesses. She designs a poster to stick up around town and asks me to scan and upload it.

I study the poster she's handed me. It looks familiar.

"Did you base this on next-door's missing cat poster?"

"What if I did?" Holly folds her arms. "They got Sheba back, didn't they? Are you going to sit there asking stupid questions or are you going to scan it for me?" Her kicking foot is swinging.

I start scanning.

We get all sorts of strange replies to the lost ~~cat~~ Dad poster. One seems promising, although it's just as odd as the others:

> I am Porter. I am 14. I have information
> about the toilet explosion and film of
> the Christmas market. I can meet you
> to discuss it, but only in your home
> and only after dark. No front doors.

"I told him to come round tonight," Holly says, showing me the email.

"To our house?" I squeak. "Are you completely mad? He's probably planning to murder us in our beds."

"Then don't go to bed. Come on, Know-All, this is important."

45

"Have you read this note, Holly? Only after dark? No front doors? What is he? Some kind of vampire? Doesn't this strike you as weird?"

"No weirder than exploding toilets and disappearing parents. Do you want to find Dad or not?"

"Of course I do."

That doesn't stop me screaming when I hear a bang later that night.

I jump straight out of bed – I don't want to take any chances – and check my phone.

22:47

I'm not tired, probably because I've been napping every afternoon this week. Something about the combination of stress and Curry in a Hurry hot chocolate always knocks me out.

Wide awake now, I tiptoe across the landing to check on Holly. Her bedroom light is off but I can make out her silhouette against the window as she lifts the latch.

"Noooooo," I yell.

But the dark figure pushes against the window and clambers over the sill. He moves towards me in the dark, lifting his right arm, brandishing a weapon. Without thinking, I rush at him and drive him backwards, knocking him off balance so he stumbles into Holly's open wardrobe. I shove his chest with a strength I didn't know I had and slam the wardrobe doors. Fingers trembling, I turn the key in the lock and trap him inside. My hands won't stop shaking.

Holly flicks on the bedroom lights and stares at me, her mouth wide open.

The wardrobe doors rattle.

"He's here," I say. "The Porter guy is here."

"Yeah. I got that."

"He's in your wardrobe."

"Yeah, got that too."

"I'm not sure what happened," I confess. "I kept thinking about him murdering us in our beds, so when he raised his arm . . ."

"You barged him into my wardrobe!" Holly's mouth twitches. "Impressive!"

"What now?" I ask as the wardrobe doors clatter.

"We'll have to let him out at some point. Might be an idea to do it now, before he kills my clothes."

Closing my eyes and taking a calming breath, I move closer to the wardrobe. "Er, hello?"

"Hello," the wardrobe replies.

"I'm going to unlock the doors and on three I want you to throw out your weapon."

"Weapon?"

"The weapon you were waving around as you climbed in the window. You ready? One . . . Two . . . Three . . ."

I open the right-hand wardrobe door, getting ready to slam it on his arm if necessary. "Throw!"

Crash!

Holly and I gaze at the 'weapon'.

Holly giggles. "Beware the deadly water bottle!"

I unlatch the left-hand door, feeling flustered. "Okay. You can come out, slowly!"

The door creaks open. A face peers out from between Holly's skinny jeans and glittery vest tops; a round, symmetrical face attached to a long neck, with skin the same creamy off-white colour as our Armitage Shanks toilet.

"Hello." Porter unfolds himself from the wardrobe and holds out his hand. "I'm Porter Lewis. Portaloo spotter."

"Huh?"

"Like a train spotter. But with fewer trains and more portable toilets." Porter's ears turn red as we stare at him. He thrusts his hand in his back pocket.

"You watch . . . toilets?" I take a step back and wonder whether we should chuck him straight back out of the window. What sort of hobby is toilet-watching for a teenage boy?

"Only portaloos. And only empty ones. They are design classics. The simple lines of the exterior and the deceptively spacious interior . . ."

"That is one freaky hobby," Holly narrows her eyes at Porter. "Although it does make you the best example, ever, for Know-All's weird collection of people whose names match what they do."

Holly's right. Porter Lewis the portaloo spotter beats Mr Payne the dentist *and* Lee King the plumber. Last week Holly tried to convince me she'd met Robin Banks the master criminal, along with his assistant, Nick de Lotte, and his brother-in-law, Robin Holmes. As if I'd believe that! Okay, maybe I did. But only for a few minutes. Until Holly fell about laughing.

What Holly doesn't understand is that Nominative Determinism is a "thing", with a Wikipedia page and everything. It's a proper theory that suggests your name can affect your job, your hobbies, even your character.

I think about names a lot. I believe there's a reason Dad's name sounds like "brain" and mine sounds like "Know-All", just as I believe Mr and Mrs Lewis decided their son's fate when they christened him Porter.

"A portaloo spotter?" I repeat. "Does that mean you know about portaloo explosions?"

Porter nods.

"There have been two unexplained toilet blasts this year: an eruption in a portaloo at an Austrian Folk Festival and the explosion at Lindon Christmas market, where I happened to be filming."

Porter's voice squeaks but I guess he's feeling awkward talking to us about the day Dad disappeared. I may have to revisit my squeaking = lying theory.

"The Austrian investigators say toilet chemicals reacted badly with a dropped cigarette at the Folk Festival." Porter frowns. "Why do people always blame the portaloo? Don't they realise portaloos are—"

"Can we stick to the point?" Holly asks. "Christmas market?"

"Right. Sorry. Got carried away. The portaloos at the Christmas market were Splendaloos. Those guys have been supplying portable toilets since 1984 and have approximately four thousand nine hundred toilets for hire. That's about the same number of toilets the Americans used when they first swore in Barack Obama as President. Americans have no respect for portaloos, you know. Tens of thousands of portaloos in the US are set on fire, spray-painted or tipped over every month. Tens of thousands! That's almost five per cent of all the toilets in use over there. It's shocking . . ."

"The point, Porter!"

"Sorry. But do you realise how much a new portaloo costs? Around five hundred pounds! Five hundred pounds! These toilets deserve our respect.

It's all in the name. Guess what they call portaloos in the United States? Portapotties! I mean. Seriously? How can you give something the appreciation it deserves when you refer to it as a portapotty? If they only knew—"

"Enough!" Holly yells. "Tell us about the Christmas market explosion."

Porter reaches into his pocket and pulls out a computer memory stick. "Why don't I show you instead?"

"Show us?" I stare at him, dry-mouthed. "You filmed the actual explosion? Give me that!"

I lunge at Porter and grab his arms. The memory stick flies through the air and lands in Holly's sock drawer. What am I supposed to do now? I don't want to hurt Porter, but I'm holding on to him and I'll look stupid if I just let go.

"I didn't film it deliberately." Porter uses his longer reach to grip my head and force me backwards, breaking my hold and trapping me at a distance.

"Ow!" he yells as I bend one of his fingers back.

"Sorry. It's a move I learnt from an anti-bullying video on YouTube," I explain.

"That's cheating. You're the one bullying me." Porter sucks his injured finger. "All I was doing was filming the new Splendamini 3000, a mini-portaloo. It's an industry revolution. I didn't realise— Oof!"

Holly wallops both of us in the ribs. We stagger apart.

"Enough!" she barks. "Porter, find that memory stick among my socks. Know-All, find us a place to watch it."

I obey, but when she turns around I stick out my tongue. I turn and catch Porter doing the same.

8

Film Footage

I stomp across the landing, kicking no-longer-seasonal Christmas decorations out of the way as I lead Holly, Porter and Porter's memory stick through the minefield of tatty tinsel and rejected Christmas tree baubles to my room. My desktop is the only place we can watch Porter's film now Fake Insurance Man has taken Dad's hard drive and laptop.

I love my computer. I love all computers. My perfect world would contain no people – just me and a million computers. Dad would probably agree about the computers but he'd keep the *clever* people in his world. He used to say that if he ruled the country he'd banish everyone with an IQ below one hundred and twenty. Holly called him an intelligence fascist, but Dad said he'd give them a chance to increase their IQ first, which is fair. Isn't it?

Anyway, that's how I got the idea for the brain ray.

Dad and I spent a lot of our free time together imagining intelligence-increasing devices. Our first idea was for a brain cap with electrodes that plunge into the key "intelligence" areas of the brain, which studies suggest are:

    i. the left prefrontal cortex (behind the forehead)
    ii. the left temporal cortex (behind the ear)
    iii. the left parietal cortex (at the top and back of the head)

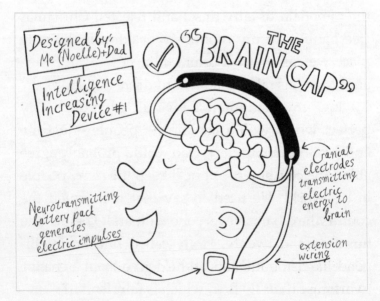

Designed by: Me (Noelle)+Dad

Intelligence Increasing Device #1

✓ "THE BRAIN CAP"

Cranial electrodes transmitting electric energy to brain

Neurotransmitting battery pack generates electric impulses

extension wiring

We rejected the brain cap pretty quickly. Dad said it was because intelligence lies in the connections between areas of the brain, not in the areas themselves. But I suspect it was because he knew we'd never convince anyone to let us drill into their skull.

My second idea was based on the fact that brains rely on electrical signals to communicate. I wondered if we could use electromagnetic energy to affect brain cells by creating an electromagnetic field.

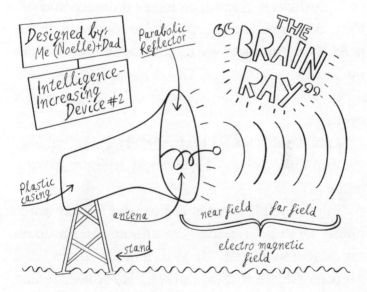

Dad liked the idea and we spent all our free time working on it.

The weird thing is I haven't thought about it much since he vanished. With Dad gone, being clever no longer seems so important. Besides, we could never figure out how to get round the dangerous side effects of electromagnetic radiation.

"Hello?" Holly waves a hand in front of my face.

"Sorry. Daydreaming." I pull open my bedroom door.

Porter's eyes widen to almost perfect circles as he spots my multi-screen computer. I'm glad people have eyelids. It is not nice to see so much eyeball. Why does nobody except Dad understand that I need six monitors to see data the way it appears in my head?

"It was a birthday present," I tell Porter's eyeballs.

"I got a doll's tea set that year," Holly grumbles.

I don't like the way Holly and Porter are looking at me.

"I didn't tell Dad what to buy, did I? And watch out for Uranus," I snap as Porter bumps his head on my Meccano planet. "It took months for me and Meccano Morris to create an accurate-scale Meccano model of the solar system for our science project. The last thing I need is you causing space to collapse in on itself."

I push Porter out of the way as the media player flickers into action. The film opens on the mini-portaloos. Porter has added a voiceover describing them. In detail.

I'm starting to wonder if anyone has ever literally died of boredom, when a man wanders into shot at the edge of the screen.

"Dad!" My hands scrabble in my bag for the scorched leather lace-ups. I lift them so they're half covering my eyes.

"Don't hide behind those stupid shoes." Holly yanks at my arm. "We need to know what happened. What has Dad got in that bag?"

I lower the shoes, but Dad has already entered the toilet and all I see are closed doors.

A few minutes later, there's movement at the far edge of the screen.

"Freeze!" I say. "Is that Dad's portaloo? Why are you moving the camera in the wrong direction?"

"Sorry," says Porter, backing away and head-butting Venus. "People get a bit funny if they think you're filming them on the toilet."

Fortunately, at that moment, the camera wobbles, giving a clearer view of Dad emerging from the portaloo.

"Where's the bag, Holly? You said Dad was carrying a bag. I don't see one."

"Seriously? You're obsessing over Dad's bag?" Holly flicks Saturn at me. "Haven't you noticed something slightly more important?"

I reattach Saturn's rings. "Like what?"

"Like the fact that Dad, who is supposed to have spontaneously combusted in a portaloo, has just come out of the portaloo! Dur!" Holly grabs Dad's shoe and hits me with it. "You're supposed to be the observant one. Look! Dad came out of the portaloo."

CLUE 11

Dad came out of the portaloo!

9

Missing

The camcorder's time code reads 15:18:04. According to the newspapers the portaloo is due to explode in one minute and fifty-six seconds, "wiping out" my dad and leaving only his smoking shoes behind. But how is that possible? Dad came out of the portaloo.

What about my theory that Dad was kidnapped? Where are the kidnappers? Where are the villains who rigged the red-herring explosion? Did the explosion even happen?

An on-screen boom answers *that* question, shaking my bedroom walls.

The camera tracks the source of the blast, zooming in on the portaloo Dad left only minutes earlier.

Black smoke belches from the toilet's air vents. Angry orange flames flicker through the gaps in the door, creating a heat haze in front of the camera.

Blurred figures run across the screen; some fleeing for safety, others fighting the fire with bottled water.

A woman wearing reindeer antlers emerges from a nearby Christmas grotto carrying a mop bucket full of water, which she throws at the toilet door. Following behind her is a red-faced, middle-aged man, squeezed into an Elf's outfit several sizes too small. He loosens his belt and rams his body against the burning portaloo. Oblivious to the smoke and the water, he smashes the toilet backwards, away from the other units, preventing the fire from spreading along the row.

"What an Elf," Porter murmurs. "What a hero."

A large crowd gathers as Super-sized Super Elf pulls his green sleeves over his hands and heaves at the portaloo door. The fire must have warped the plastic, moulding the door shut, because it's not shifting. People push and shove to get a better view. I feel squashed just watching them elbow each other and press in together. The door finally breaks free and the mob pushes forwards, united by one common goal – to look inside.

There is a mass groan and I can hear people gagging as the stench hits them.

Porter's camcorder zooms in and I repeat Holly's words: "Dad came out of the portaloo. Dad came out of the portaloo. Dad came out of the portaloo."

It's the only way I can keep Vigil-Aunty's carrot casserole down.

The poo-plastered, blood-splattered cubicle looks like something from one of Holly's horror movies. Dark reddish-brown gloop covers everything: seeping from the plastic walls; squelching on to the loo roll fires burning on the U-shaped toilet seat; splattering the soot-streaked, water-drenched bag at the back of the portaloo and the splintered glass on the ground.

Projectile poo – the result of many visits by many bottoms over many hours – has exploded on to the ceiling, walls and door. People back away, covering their mouths and noses, avoiding puddles of water and vomit. There's blood everywhere. But whose? PC Eric says they found Dad's blood at the scene, but if Dad wasn't there, where did it come from? And who dropped that glass on the floor?

The microphone picks up the sound of Porter retching, but he manages to hold the camera steady as the emergency services arrive. Uniformed police order everyone back and cordon off the nearby roads and alleyways with thick yellow tape. Porter follows their instructions and moves away, but the zoom function on his camera allows him to capture the action. The volume is muted but we can still hear what's happening.

Super-sized Super Elf pushes past the policemen and police cordons. "What's going on? And what's that bag doing in there? How can a person explode, but not their bag?"

"Polybenzimidazole," I mutter.

"Bless you!" says Porter.

"No. That's what the bag's made of. It's a fire-resistant fabric. I remember Dad ordering it online. He said it would be cool to have a fireproof bag."

"Cool . . . and convenient," Holly says.

"Where are Dad's shoes?" I ask. "I thought they were all that was left after the explosion."

As if on cue, a man in a crinkly white suit and blue rubber gloves brushes small slivers of glass off the Polybenzimidazole bag and unzips it to reveal a pair of familiar-looking brown lace-ups. He loosens the laces to get a better view of the name printed inside.

"See?" Holly says. "Convenient! You should be writing this in your stupid notebook."

CLUE 12

Dad left a fireproof bag in an exploding toilet.

I squint at the screen. Something's wrong. The shoes in my hand are scorched and stained, whereas the shoes on the screen seem completely unharmed.

With an unprofessional grunt, the crime scene examiner wipes a splat of ceiling poo from his forehead. The movement overbalances him and he slips on wet, bloodstained glass, landing on the toilet and dropping the shoes into one of the little loo roll fires that are still burning between the puddles on the floor. He whips the lace-ups out the fire, wipes off the poo, and rubs at the burn marks on the leather uppers.

I stroke the identical marks on the shoe I'm holding and realise I should probably wash my hands.

The camera zooms out and an ill-looking policeman appears in front of the cordon. He demands that everyone hand over their cameras. The screen goes dark. Dark but wavy. Like a close-up of the threads inside a coat pocket.

I glance at Porter.

His face turns pink. "I didn't want to lose my footage of the Splendaloo mini-model. I didn't realise. The minute I saw your message I got in touch. You have to understand . . ."

"I don't have to understand anything. You let everyone believe my dad died in that explosion." My words fill the room. I want to scream into the silence that follows.

"You have to show that to the police," I tell Porter, shoving my hands into my pockets to suppress the urge to throttle him. "When they see Dad didn't blow up, they'll help me find out what happened. It doesn't make sense. If Dad didn't explode then where did all that blood come from? Could there have been a smaller blast while Dad was out of shot? Maybe he was injured and wandered on to the streets, dazed and confused."

"What about the bag?" Holly asks.

"People forget things when they're concussed," I tell her. But it's harder to come up with an explanation for the shoes.

Holly shakes her head. "And I suppose Dad carried a spare pair of shoes around in case of unexpected footwear emergencies?"

"Yes! What you said. Spare shoes." I jump up and down, pulling Holly with me. "Dad's alive! We just need to work out where he went. He could be wandering the streets with no memory, waiting for us to find him."

"If he has no memory, he won't remember us, so he won't be waiting for us to do anything." Holly pulls her hands free and ejects the memory stick. "What if he doesn't want to be found?"

"Of course he wants to be found," I say. "We'll start where he disappeared. You told me they're setting up a Valentine's market in the same place as the Christmas market. Come on, Holly. This is our chance."

"The Valentine's market?" Holly says with the enthusiasm of a stepped-on snail. "How do you suggest we get to Lindon now Mum's permanently attached to the sofa?"

"We take the train."

"You? On a train?" Holly scoffs. "You've spent your life with your head buried in science books. I bet you don't even know how to buy a ticket."

Porter stands, carefully avoiding dangling planets and poo-shoes. "I'm taking the one-twenty to Lindon on Friday. Why don't you come with me?"

"During school hours?" I can't hide my shock.

"Nice." Holly brightens up. "We'll meet you at the station, Porter. One-fifteen, Friday."

10

Lies

I can't believe we're skipping school. What if someone sees us in town? What if someone doesn't see us in school? What if I miss something important? What if I fail my exams?

"Stop thinking!" Holly says sternly. "And what *are* you wearing?"

My sister has no taste. My brown corduroy skirt and jacket (with orange leather elbow patches) are perfect. Not only do they provide warmth and comfort, but they're also similar to the suit Dad was wearing when he disappeared. (Not the skirt, obviously. Dad doesn't wear skirts. Except that one time in Spain when Mum made him wear her sarong because his Speedos were too small. But I don't think that counts.)

I'm hoping the outfit will jog people's memories. I do seem to be attracting attention, but that may be because of the scorched lace-ups I'm wearing round my neck.

We find Porter, who takes one look at my shoe necklace and shakes his head.

"Lose the shoes," Holly says, shoving us onto the Lindon train and finding me a plastic bag.

I place the shoes in the bag and make sure I keep them close during the journey, until the train pulls in at Lindon station and Holly gives us another shove.

"Brrr," I grumble, rubbing my arms as we head out into the street. The Met Office says the average minimum temperature in Lindon in February is 1.2 degrees centigrade, but this is definitely colder. I can see my breath in the air and that's only good if you're a fire-breathing dragon. I gaze longingly at the warm(ish) station building.

Porter tugs the strings on his hood so it covers his face.

"Portaloos that way." He points up the steep hill.

I groan and wonder if I'll ever be warm again.

"It might help us figure out what happened if we go through what we know about the Christmas market," Holly suggests as we climb the hill.

I scan my frostbitten brain. "We know over three hundred thousand people visited last year. We know when it began there were only eleven stalls, but last year there were more than two hundred and fifty. We know—"

Holly yawns. I try and think of something that isn't yawn-worthy. Nothing. Except . . .

"We know Dad hated the Christmas market."

"We do?" Holly stops yawning.

I nod. "Dad said he admired Oliver Cromwell's attempts to ban all Christmas celebrations and wished, every year, for a contemporary Cromwell to come along. But not before he got the chance to blow up the tannoy system and cyber-massacre Jingle, the Christmas market Twitter-elf."

Holly raises an eyebrow. "I suppose I should be glad he only wanted to kill a *virtual* elf."

"He said the carol singers would be no great loss either. But I think he was joking."

"Ho, ho, ho!" Holly mutters. "I don't get it. I mean, why would someone who hates Christmas call their kids Holly and Noelle?"

"Mum must have overruled him."

Holly frowns. "Can you remember Mum overruling Dad about anything? It doesn't say much about how important we are to him if our names are the only thing he gave way on, does it?"

"It explains why he always calls me Know-All."

Holly kicks a frost-covered hedge. "He calls me Holly."

11

Talking Shoes

Valentine's Market outdoors is even worse than regular outdoors. The air tastes of cremated chestnuts and sick people's sneezes; the harsh wind feels like a thousand pins being stabbed into my face; and in the hour we've been walking, my toes have been crushed by designer pushchairs, mobility scooters and fast-moving pensioners desperate to grab their free heart-shaped loo roll covers. I'm starting to understand Dad's hatred of the tannoy system too. The constant announcements about the history of the marketplace make my teeth hurt and I wish someone would fix that stupid hissing sound.

The plastic bag with the shoes is getting heavy too. I should have left them around my neck. They were more comfortable there. I hoist the bag higher under my arm.

"Losers quit when they're tired. Winners quit when they've won."

I scowl at Porter. "I am not quitting. And knowing all about portaloos doesn't make you a winner."

"Never said it did." Porter rubs his ankles after a particularly vicious mobility scooter attack.

"Then who said it?" I whirl round.

"Said what?" Holly shoves me forward.

"That thing about winners and losers."

Holly and Porter look blank.

"I'm hearing voices. That can't be good." I reach into the plastic bag to stroke Dad's shoes. They make me feel calmer.

"Don't let others drag you down."

I slam the bag shut. Impossible! The voice is coming from inside. But that's ridiculous. The bag's empty except for the shoes.

"Don't stop here, idiot." Holly points up the hill. "We're on the main route to the cathedral. We'll be trampled to death by a herd of over-sixties."

She has a point. A large cloud of blue-rinsed hair is drifting towards us. But I can't move.

"Dad's shoes are talking to me," I murmur. "*Isaac Newton!* Am I having a mental breakdown?"

"Talking shoes?" Holly grabs the bag, accidentally bumping into two sweet-looking old ladies. Holly tries to apologise but the grannies are having

71

none of it. One raises her cane to rap Holly's ankles as the other mutters about "young people today". On the plus side, Holly's new image as a granny-basher creates more space around us.

Holly opens the plastic bag. "What did they say?"

"It's not enough to have a good mind," the shoes hiss. *"The important thing is to use it. Nobody remembers who came in second. The first man gets the oyster; the second man gets the shell . . ."*

That doesn't even make sense. I tried an oyster once and it tasted like snot, whereas shells are shiny and sound like the sea.

"Dad's shoes are mean," Holly says, dumping them on the nearest wall.

Thank *Zuckerberg*! Holly heard them too! I'm not mad. Or maybe we both are. Could it be genetic? I need to find out if Porter can hear them too.

Holly glances at her watch. "It's half-four. Isn't this nap time?"

"Ha ha."

"I'm serious. Don't you think the timing is odd? You nap at the same time every day for a week and that's the exact time the shoes start chatting." Holly waves a talking shoe at me. "This sounds like a recorded message. What if it plays at the same time every day?"

"I wouldn't know, would I? I'm asleep."

"You can't always be asleep. Surely sometimes you just lie there?"

"Nope. Always asleep. It must be all the effort I'm putting into finding Dad."

"That or something someone's putting into your Curry in a Hurry hot chocolate." Holly shivers as the temperature drops further.

"Shhh," Porter says. "The shoes are talking again."

So Porter can hear them. That has to be a good thing.

"Keep these shoes close in memory of your father."

"Unbelievable!" Holly picks up one of Dad's shoes and bashes the other with it. "Can't you see what's going on, Know-All? You're being brainwashed!"

"Work hard," the shoes squeak as Holly smashes the one in her hand against the one on the wall. *"W-w-w-work . . . h-h-ha-ha-aaarrrgghhh . . ."*

"You killed the talking shoes." Porter looks impressed.

"Mercy killing," Holly says.

Porter grins. "Death penalty!"

"Brainwashed?" I say slowly. "You think I'm being brainwashed?"

Holly nods.

"Like a prisoner of war?"

"Yeah," Holly says. "Except you're not a prisoner and you're not at war."

"And you think they're putting something into my hot chocolate," I say. "You mean drugs, don't you? You think I'm a non-imprisoned, non-warring prisoner of war *who has been drugged*!"

Who would do something like that?

CLUE 13
Someone installed a recorded message in Dad's shoes and (might have) drugged me so I'd hear it in my sleep.

12

Blood Stains

I don't notice Porter has stopped moving until I walk into the back of him. When I look up, I see a row of portable toilets. They're familiar from Porter's film, but bigger than they seemed on-screen. A quick scan tells me they're approximately ninety centimetres wide and two hundred and ten centimetres tall. The numbers are familiar. I flick through the images in my brain until I figure out why. They're from a maths problem I was given for extra homework a few months back.

The question gave variables like detonation velocity and material density, and asked what quantity of a particular explosive would be required to blow up a lightweight plastic box measuring ninety by ninety by one hundred and twenty centimetres.

That wasn't a hypothetical maths question box. It was a non-hypothetical plastic toilet.

CLUE 14
I was tricked into calculating
how to blow up a portaloo.

Why didn't I figure this out earlier? Ms Grimm is right about me being unable to connect maths to real life.

Ms Grimm!

Ms Grimm set the extra homework. She's back as my number one suspect. The woman is obsessed with blowing things up.

Thinking hard, I trip on a pile of rubbish and fall hard, cutting my hand on broken glass. I clutch my hand against my chest.

"Help!" I whimper.

Porter starts texting, hopefully summoning emergency medical assistance.

Holly prises my fingers open and rolls her eyes at me. "I think your vital organs can still function without that millilitre of blood."

I glance down and see a small scratch instead of the gaping wound I was expecting. Why don't my injuries ever look as gruesome as they feel? And why am I so dizzy?

Staggering to my feet, I stumble towards the road, desperate to escape the portaloos. My head is full of black smoke belching from air vents.

Holly and Porter call my name. I can hear them running behind me but I don't slow down.

Ow! My hand stings. I remember the online medical journal entry about "First Aid for Cuts and Scrapes". It said, *"Raise the wounded part of the body above the heart to slow the bleeding"*. Perhaps my blood vessels are frozen. Who knows what will happen when I get back in the warm and they defrost? I raise my arm in the air just in case.

A taxi pulls over. I try to explain that I wasn't signalling but Porter dives into the cab and pulls me and Holly in behind him. I protest at first, but once I'm in that warm interior, my protests die down.

The driver growls when he sees me cradling my hand. "Bleed in here and it's a fifty quid clean-up fee. This is the second time some fool's bled all over my cab. You even look like the Christmas market guy, just younger and with less facial hair, which probably comes from being a child. And a girl."

"You called me a fool," I protest. "I'm not a fool. I have an IQ of a hundred and fifty se—"

"Shut up, Know-All." Holly peers around the front seat at the driver. "Who did you say she looked like?"

"Like the fella that bled all over the cab after the Christmas market. Except that guy's foot was bleeding, not his hand. Served him right for wearing flip-flops. Who wears flip-flops in winter? Where were the guy's shoes?"

Ah! Now I understand why Holly's so interested.

CLUE 15

After the portaloo explosion, a
taxi driver picked up someone
matching Dad's description.

"Do you remember where you took him?" Porter asks.

"It was months ago," I point out. "Of course he doesn't—"

"Grey building, up by Lindon castle," the taxi driver says. His voice squeaks, but why would a taxi driver lie?

"Who was with him?" I ask. "One person? A group? Man or woman? What did they look like?"

"Slow down," the cabbie protests. "I can't remember the details. Like you say, it was months ago." He's squeaking again. What's he hiding?

"Can you take us to the place you dropped him?"

The driver strokes his chin. "One drop of blood and there's trouble."

Holly glances at my hand. "She's already lost her drop for today. Let's go."

"How much is this going to cost?" I'm worried about my calculator money.

"I'll pay," Porter offers.

Holly and I stare at him in surprise. Porter looks at his feet. The taxi driver nods and pulls out into the traffic. As his sleeve rides up his arm, I spot a flash of turquoise. I shake my head. What is it with that colour?

13

Grim Statue

I recognise the route the taxi's taking. We used to come this way with Mum all the time. Her favourite shoe shop is on the right as we pull up outside the castle walls next to a large grey stone building.

I buzz down the window and stare at the sign above the double doors.

Lindon-based Opportunities for the Superior
Education of Remarkable Students

I nod in approval and wonder why Holly's giggling.

"You're sure this is the right place?"

"Positive." The cabbie points at the petrol station across the road. "That's where I cleaned up the blood. Couldn't get it all out, mind. You can see the stain on the carpets."

"Nice." Holly doesn't even glance down.

But I'm mesmerised by the faded proof that Dad might have sat here and may still be close.

"Come on." Holly shoves me from behind. "Out!"

I open the car door and I'm hit by a blast of cold air.

"Holly, are you sure it was Dad?" I ask, clinging to the warmth of the taxi.

"Who else would be wandering around the Christmas market without any shoes, looking like an older, blokeier version of you?"

Holly has a point. So does her elbow, which she uses to force me out on to the pavement. I stumble into Porter, who's frozen in place like a videogame avatar that's had its last action cancelled.

Side-stepping to avoid him, I bump into the ugliest statue I've ever seen – a misshapen, yet oddly familiar, grey-stone woman with lopsided features, bulgy eyes and a tiny, angry mouth that makes her look like she has just sat on a wasp. The statue is new. There's no way we could have missed something this hideous when we came here with Mum.

I study the plaque at the bottom:

MALLORY GRIMM
FOUNDER OF
L.O.S.E.R.S

Who she?

Pythagoras!

CLUE 16

An ugly concrete version of my maths
teacher is perched on a plinth in the
place where Dad was last seen.

This must be the other school where Ms Grimm
teaches. PC Eric didn't explain she'd founded it as
well. Strange that it's beside Mum's favourite shoe
shop. Stranger still that it's in the exact spot Dad
may have been dropped off after the explosion.

Strangest of all that Porter and I were picked up by the same driver who dropped Dad off.

What are the chances?

My brain tingles. There's something about the plaque. Something I should be noticing. I just need a minute. It'll come to me.

"Hawkins?" A familiar voice grates across my thoughts. "What are you doing here?"

Ms Grimm! In the flesh, lurking behind her greystone twin.

I look at my feet. I look at the sky. I look at the gloomy, grey school for the gifted. I look everywhere except at Ms Grimm, which is how I spot the silhouette at a second-floor school window. I'm too far away to see clearly, but it looks like a male figure signalling to someone, or something, over my shoulder. Then, just as suddenly, he's gone, vanishing behind a curtain as Ms Grimm whirls to see what caught my attention.

I check whether Holly or Porter saw the mysterious figure. No. Holly's too busy watching me and Porter is nowhere to be seen. He's slipped away into the shadows, vanishing as hastily as the face in the window. The taxi driver has disappeared too. Ms Grimm seems to have that effect on people.

"Hawkins? I'm talking to you," Ms Grimm snaps. "What are you doing here?"

"Um. Sightseeing?"

"You don't sound very sure."

"This is a lovely statue," I blurt in desperation. "What an honour for you."

"Ah, well . . ." The hard line of Ms Grimm's mouth softens. "The school's financial backers thought it would be a good idea."

"And you founded a school for remarkable students. How amazing!"

Ms Grimm purrs.

"And you called it LOSERS?" Holly sniggers.

The purr becomes a growl. Ms Grimm points to the sign on the grey stone building. "No. I called it 'Lindon-based Opportunities for the Superior Education of Remarkable Students'."

"L . . . O . . . S . . . E . . . R . . . S . . . LOSERS." Holly grins. "What's so remarkable about your students, anyway? I bet they're the usual top-set types – freaks and robots."

"Oi!" I protest. "I'm in top set. So what does that make me? A freak? Or a robot?"

Until yesterday I'd have gone with popular opinion and said freak, but I can't get the hissing shoes out of my mind. What if I'm a robot, programmed to behave in a particular way?

Perhaps the answer is a Venn diagram with the set of freaks in one circle, the set of robots in the other and me in the overlapping bit in the middle. Noelle Hawkins – freak *and* robot.

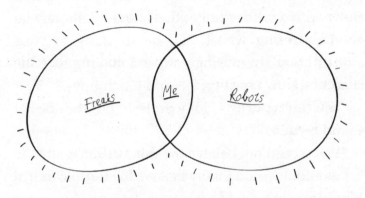

I don't get a chance to share my theory with Holly because Ms Grimm's growl has become a roar. She grabs Holly by the collar and forces her into the back of a nearby black Honda Civic.

I dive in behind my sister, worried Ms Grimm is going to shout her to death and then dump the body in a dark alley. I glance around for Porter. Still no sign.

"Insolent child," Ms Grimm screeches, slamming into the driver's seat and accelerating away from the kerb. "I'm taking you home."

"Home?" That's it? No dark alleys. My heart rate slows slightly. But only slightly. How would Ms Grimm react if I asked her, politely, to look at the road instead of glaring at Holly?

"You need taking in hand." Ms Grimm pokes Holly with a witchy finger that should definitely be on the steering wheel. "I'll be speaking to your mother about grounding you, and making sure the head keeps you in at breaks and lunchtimes."

"You can't do that," Holly protests, but she doesn't sound certain.

"You would not believe the things I can do."

I would. I would totally believe the terrible things Ms Grimm can do. I shudder as she turns her attention to me. But she's calmer now.

"You, Hawkins, are a different story. Easily led astray, but a brilliant mind. I am delighted to see you showing such an interest in my organisation—"

"Cyclist," I squeak. "Watch out for the cyclist."

Ms Grimm swerves sharply, nearly hitting a lamp post.

"She's going to invite you to join her freak show," Holly hisses in my ear while Ms Grimm is distracted. "You have to say yes!"

"Where was I?" Ms Grimm says.

"You were wrapping us around a lamp post," Holly replies.

Ms Grimm ignores her. "Ah yes, Hawkins, we were discussing your interest in LOSERS. I've been considering this for a while and I have decided to enrol you in my school. You will need to be ready for collection at two p.m. on Sunday – Bah! Idiot!"

I flinch. Then I realise she's shouting at a pedestrian who's been foolish enough to stand on the pavement she's just mounted.

Holly hisses in my ear, "This is the perfect opportunity for us to get inside the LOSERS building."

Hmmm. What's all this "us" business? This isn't us, this is me, and that is *not* how I imagined the investigation going. I pictured Holly doing most of the brave bits with me taking more of a desk-based-investigator role.

"You have three days to gather your things," Ms Grimm says, hitting a signpost with her wing mirror. "You must be terribly excited."

I must? Then why do I feel so sick?

14

Under Surveillance

Twenty-three hours and counting until LOSERS come to take me away. What am I supposed to pack? How can I conduct my investigation or contact Holly without my computer? And why is there a loud speaker attached to the front door?

"GET BACK IN THE HOUSE, SPAWN OF SATAN!" the speaker growls as Holly decides to forget she's grounded again.

The electronic voice has been going off every few hours, since Ms Grimm dumped us home last night. It sounds like something from the age-inappropriate *Terminator* film Uncle Max brought round last week – evil and robotic, as if a hundred murderous machines are yelling at once.

"It's probably an automated response triggered

every time we open the front door," I reassured Holly the first time it went off.

Holly, being Holly, tested my theory by clambering over the Christmas lights and straddling the sill of the bay window.

"BEHAVE YOURSELF, SCRUFFBUCKET, OR SUFFER THE CONSEQUENCES!" Terminator Voice boomed. "AND TIE YOUR SHOELACES!"

Terminator Voice has a sense of humour. This morning, when Smokin' Joe tried to hide beneath the front hedge, Terminator Voice bellowed, "I CAN SEEEEEEEEE YOU." When Smokin' Joe loped off down the road, Terminator Voice called after him, "RUN, FAT BOY, RUN!"

I grin at the memory.

"Hey, Spawn of Satan," I call as Holly slams the door.

She throws a reindeer cushion at me. "Just because you never want to leave the house doesn't mean we all like living in a prison. That voice is evil. How can it see us?"

"That's obvious."

CLUE 17

Someone has installed CCTV
cameras around our home.

But who? And why? Surely Ms Grimm wouldn't go to all this trouble?

One thing is clear. Holly's going crazy under house arrest. I don't blame her. I just wish she wouldn't take her excess energy out on me.

"Ow!" I yell. "I like to have fun as much as the next person, Holly, but if you ninja-jump onto my back one more time I'll . . . I'll . . . I'll lock myself in the bathroom."

I need space to think. I've finally worked out what was bothering me about the plaque beneath Ms Grimm's statue. It came to me while I was staring at the portrait of Dad, trying to figure out the strange note in his hand. My eyes were drawn to that blanked-out word:

L _ _ _ _ S?

Eureka!

CLUE 18

The missing word on Dad's
painting is LOSERS –
the name of Ms Grimm's school for the gifted.

I grab Holly. "Look! This proves there's a connection between Dad and the Remarkable Students' building."

Holly is less impressed than she should be. "We already knew that."

"We suspected it," I correct her. "Now we have proof."

Holly yawns. "One of your many problems, Know-All, is you waste too much time proving things you already know. Now, if that's all, I need to get to work. The back door is under surveillance but I'm pretty sure the cameras don't cover the back yard or the kitchen. So I'm digging a tunnel to emerge near the gate."

"Great plan. Definitely not a waste of time. It only took eighty odd prisoners eleven months to tunnel out of Stalag Luft III in World War II."

Holly's recoils as if I've suggested Santa's a kitten smuggler.

I feel bad. "On the bright side, it worked a treat for Fantastic Mr Fox."

That's enough to encourage Holly.

While my sister smashes kitchen floor tiles with a corkscrew, I go up to my room to check out LOSERS' website. It doesn't say much – it's really just a slide show of attractive, clever-looking teenagers doing attractive, clever-looking things. I stare at one of the photographs.

Is that . . . ?

No, it can't be. For a minute I thought it was a picture of Porter, but that's ridiculous. Isn't it?

The attractive yet slightly toilet-like face disappears as LOSERS' mission statement flashes over the top.

"To increase the intelligence of bright young people and contribute to the betterment of society as a whole."

What's interesting is what the website *doesn't* show. No list of staff. No contact details. No record of the people in authority.

" G R R R R R R R R R R R R R - G - G - G - G - GRRRRRRRRRRRRRRRRRRRRRRRRRRRR."

I jump up, smashing my knees beneath my desk. *Tim Berners-Lee!*

What is that roaring sound? It rises to a whine and then deepens to a throaty grind. Holly must have raided the garage for tools to help with the tunnelling. Don't tell me she found a pneumatic drill?

"STOP THAT, THIS INSTANT!" Terminator Voice might not be able to see Holly, but it can obviously hear the racket she's making.

I shut my bedroom door to muffle the lunacy and continue my internet search. Unfortunately, Google can't tell me any more about LOSERS or why those letters were written on the picture. I give my six computer monitors a pat and stroke my Meccano solar system. Why can't I stay here, at home? Why do I have to go to this mysterious school? I'm not one of those people who dream of adventure. I'm more the type that dreams of non-adventure.

I wince as the mechanical whining becomes a steady roar. Holly must have wandered into camera shot because Terminator Voice thunders, "HOLLY HAWKINS, PUT THAT CHAINSAW DOWN!"

15

Poster Boy

The driver opens the sliding door of LOSERS' van and glances at his watch while I take Holly through my list of Things to Remember While I'm Away.

> #1: *DO NOT use the chainsaw.*
> #2: *DO keep an eye on Mum – especially her nosebleeds.*

I squint through the front window and wave at the back of Mum's head. She turns slightly and for a moment I think she might make eye contact, but the moment passes and she burrows deeper into the sofa.

The driver helps me into the van, explaining that the eleven Remarkable Students inside are on their way back from a field trip to a nuclear power plant.

They have paired off, leaving the person no one else wants to sit by up front, reading a book. That doesn't mean there's anything wrong with that person. That person is usually me.

The unwanted student turns and I see it's not a book he's reading – it's a catalogue of portaloo toilets and accessories.

Porter Lewis!

CLUE 19

Porter is a student at LOSERS.

"Porter? What are you –?"

"Shhh." Porter puts his finger to his lips.

"Why?"

Why didn't Porter say he was a student at LOSERS? "What happened to you on Thursday?"

"Shhh," he hisses again. "Talk about something different."

"Maybe I don't want to talk to you at all." I pull out my mobile phone and text Holly, using textspeak in case anyone's looking over my shoulder.

UR nvr gonna geS hu iz n d LUSRs bus . . . Porter! smTIN wErd goin on.

I can't believe it. I was right. Toilet-faced Porter

was one of the attractive, clever-looking students I saw on LOSERS' website.

"I need a ruler."

"Why?" Porter asks.

Oops. Didn't realise I said that out loud. Well, he did ask me to talk about something different.

"You are abnormally photogenic," I say. "I want to measure your face to see if it matches the rules of proportion."

Perfect face

Porter's face

Someone sniggers behind me and a paper aeroplane lands in my lap. I unfold it and find a leaflet advertising LOSERS, with Porter's face plastered across it.

No wonder the other Remarkable Students are avoiding him – Porter is LOSERS' poster boy.

Porter screws up the leaflet.

"Abnormally photogenic?" He pulls a curl, which immediately springs back into place. "Not with this hair."

"The hair's part of it. It makes you look like Michelangelo's statue of David." *Crossed with a toilet,* I think, but I manage not to say that bit out loud. "With clothes on, of course. It would be weird otherwise. Plus, he had a very small . . ."

The sniggers get louder. This might be a good time to stop talking.

No one says much for the rest of the journey. The other Remarkable Students are probably quiet because they're thinking remarkable thoughts. I'm quiet because I can't think of anything remarkable to say and I don't want to continue the naked-statue conversation.

As we scramble out of the minibus, I notice the name tag on Porter's bag: "Porter Grimm". Grimm? I thought he was Porter Lewis?

Porter catches me staring. "Not such a Greek statue any more?"

"*Greek* statue?" Going into Know-All mode helps me stay calm. "Michelangelo's David isn't a Greek statue. It was sculpted during the Renaissance.

Surely the Face of LOSERS should know something like that?"

Disturbed by the hurt expression on Porter's face, I walk straight into the huge grey statue. "Oof!"

Ms Grimm looks even grimmer in the twilight, up there on her pedestal, glaring down at me.

"Watch out for Mother," Porter warns.

"Mother?! *Copernicus!*" This is worse than I thought.

"Copper . . . whats?"

"Renaissance mathematician and astronomer who proposed that the Earth moves round the sun," I mutter absently. "Ms Grimm's your mother? Seriously?"

Porter nods and does an impressive impersonation of Ms Grimm. "'I'm so proud of my school, I even enrolled my son.'"

As if on cue, the huge double doors swing open, revealing the Grimm Reaper (Holly's new name for her) in all her gory glory. I scan her face for similarities to Porter and find none. Where Porter is all symmetry and toilet-bowl curves, Ms Grimm is sharp and pointy with protruding eyeballs that make her look as though someone's tried to strangle her with the tassels of her ugly velvet cloak. The dark cape and chalky-white skin give the impression she's just walked off the set of a Halloween movie and is simply counting the hours before returning to the undead.

She pulls out a box labelled MOBILES and demands our phones.

Before I put mine inside, I send a quick text to Holly: *U wont BLEv dis. TGR iz Porters mum!*

16

Picking Sides

"You lied about your surname," I hiss at Porter. "On top of everything else I'm going to have to delete you from my database."

"I didn't lie – Lewis was my dad's name," Porter hisses back as Ms Grimm leads us down a long turquoise corridor.

"Whatever."

"He's dead now."

I feel bad about the "whatever". "Sorry," I mumble.

"Don't be. I never met him."

"Oh." I'm not sure what to say so I stare at the walls. The internet says turquoise has a calming effect. The internet lies. I grow less calm with every step.

Turquoise Curry in a Hurry boxes, turquoise Kazinsky Electronics vans, turquoise iPods, turquoise-bracelet-wearing taxi drivers and now turquoise LOSERS. Surely there has to be a connection. Dad says it's not paranoia if they really are out to get you.

I stare at the non-calming turquoise walls and realise:

CLUE 20

The quotes on LOSERS' walls have the
same winning theme as the ramblings
of Dad's (now squished) shoes.

I read the quotations as we pass. Some make me feel ready to take on the world:

*Only a man who knows what it is like to be
defeated can reach down to the bottom of his
soul and come up with the extra ounce of power
it takes to win when the match is even.*
Muhammad Ali

Some make me laugh:

> *If winning isn't important, why keep score?*
> Star Trek: The Next Generation

And some are probably supposed to make me laugh, but don't:

> *There's nothing to winning, really. That is, if*
> *you happen to be blessed with a keen eye, an*
> *agile mind, and no scruples whatsoever.*
> Alfred Hitchcock

I don't like that one. Without scruples to tell us the right things to do, people would be murdering, stealing and talking with their mouths full all over the place.

Ms Grimm leads us past glass doors showing book-lined classrooms and whiteboards covered in equations. We march along yet more turquoise corridors where open doors reveal smaller, cosier rooms equipped with tablet computers, Smart Boards and the latest gadgets. At the end of a final walkway we reach the dormitory block: girls on the ground floor, boys on the floor above, staff up at the top.

There's a huge sitting room next to the girls' dorms on the ground floor. It's a Know-All's paradise: sleek, modern and full of computing equipment. I count fifteen laptops and nine games consoles hooked up to plasma screens. The tables are piled high with gadgets and techy magazines.

Ms Grimm stops just inside the door and rests her hands on Porter's shoulders. She's scarier than a sabre-toothed spider, but the gesture reminds me of pre-explosion Mum and makes my throat scratchy. She introduces me to the other Remarkable Students and everyone mumbles a quick "hello".

Ms Grimm seizes the opportunity for a motivational speech. "As you all know, you've been selected as the brightest young people in this area. Your only limits are those you place on yourself. We are here to help you remove these limits and achieve your full potential. I am so confident of what my school can achieve, I even enrolled my son."

She sounds so much like Porter's impression that I start to laugh. Unfortunately, the noise that comes out of my mouth sounds more like a donkey being strangled. Ms Grimm glares at me and I chew through my cheeks trying to keep my face straight. Porter comes to my rescue, slapping me on the back and telling everyone I must be choking with excitement at the thought of achieving my full potential.

Ms Grimm reduces her glare to half-power.

"I didn't know you had a son, Ms Grimm," I say afterwards, as the other girls escape to the dormitory.

Porter stiffens. Interesting.

Ms Grimm puts a bony arm around his shoulder. "Porter, meet Hawkins. Hawkins, meet my son, Porter."

"Oh, we've already met. I just didn't realise he was your son."

The Grimm Reaper's bulgy eyes bulge further. Porter steps on my toe. Hard. So he doesn't want his mother to know he came to see us? Even more interesting.

"We were sitting next to each other on the bus," I explain. "We had a fascinating conversation about portable toilets."

Porter's shoulders relax. Ms Grimm turns away, losing interest. With a grateful smile, Porter heads for the stairs. I pick up my bags and carry them through to the dormitory.

It's a big room – ten beds on one side, ten on the other. Behind the headboard of each bed is a small cubicle containing a desk, a chest of drawers and a wardrobe. I poke the mattress. Nice and firm. Shame about the turquoise duvet cover.

I'd expected a room full of teenage girls to be plastered with pictures of half-naked, floppy-haired boy celebrities I'm supposed to recognise. To my relief, the dorm walls are covered in astronomy charts and Higgs boson posters. Einstein smiles down from several of my dorm-mates' walls.

Ms Grimm's school is clearly doing well. Every cubicle is occupied.

Except mine.

"Has this bed always been empty?" I ask the girl beside me.

Her eyes flit around the room as though they're tracking a distressed moth. She doesn't answer.

I remember Holly's advice about not firing questions at people until we've built a rapport. I'm not sure what a rapport is, but I try a smile. It feels wonky.

I plough on. "Hello, my name's Noelle. What's yours?"

"Aisha," the girl says softly.

That went well. What am I supposed to say next? *Archimedes!* This is a social minefield. What's wrong with asking questions anyway?

"So Aisha, has this bed always been empty?"

Aisha points to a piece of A4 paper stuck on the wall behind me.

THE GREAT LEADER'S GOLDEN RULES

1. Shake off your limits and be the best you can be
2. Take pride in the school
3. Do not question the Great Leader
4. Do not indulge in idle chit-chat
5. Insert text here

"'Do not indulge in idle chit-chat'," Aisha says. "Golden Rule number four."

"I like rule number five best."

The Great Leader clearly needs help with the Golden Rules template.

"Would you like to discuss Einstein's Theory of Relativity instead?" Aisha asks politely.

"Er. Not right now. Maybe later. So who's this Great Leader?"

"Do not question the Great Leader. Golden Rule number three."

"I'm not questioning the Great Leader. I'm questioning *you* about the Great Leader. That's different."

Aisha looks like she's about to cry.

"Forget it." I retreat into the cubicle and hang up my clothes. So much for rapport.

"Her name was Gemma." Aisha's whisper carries through a small hole in the back of the wardrobe. "The girl here before you. Gemma Gold. They say she went home last week. But her comfort blanket's still here and she can't sleep without it."

"Do you think—?"

A bell rings in the distance and Aisha flees, leaving me staring at the grubby bit of blue cloth tied round my bed frame. Is this the comfort blanket she was talking about? Ugh. If it's a clue, it's a heavily sucked one.

So who *is* this Great Leader? Is that what Ms Grimm calls herself here? I look at the Golden Rules poster.

I don't like number one: Shake off your limits.

Limits, like scruples, are a good thing. I tried to explain this to Vigil-Aunty when we got pulled over for speeding. If the traffic police couldn't punish her for breaking the speed limit then they'd have to follow her around until she caused a proper accident (which was inevitable given the way she was driving). I think Vigil-Aunty got the point – we haven't been pulled over since. Although, come to think of it, she hasn't given me a lift since.

What worries me is that if someone with no limits has kidnapped Dad, there's no saying what they might do to him.

17

LOSERS´ Routine

7:45	Run up and down stairs five times *because* exercise enhances brain function by increasing blood flow to the brain. *(If it doesn't kill you first.)*
8:00	Breakfast: herrings and green leafy vegetables *because* oily fish contain Omega-3 fatty acids that improve the performance of brain cell membranes. *(So why are there no penguins on Mastermind?)*
8:30	Chess Hour *because* chess encourages you to use both sides of your brain, improving critical thinking and visualisation skills. *(Not when your opponent has herring breath.)*

9:30	Maths Hour *because* solving maths puzzles improves your ability to learn, concentrate and reason. *(Not when some of your classmates are still crying about losing chess.)*
10:30	Music Hour *because* studies show music lessons in childhood lead to better exam results later. *(Because parents who force their children to learn instruments also force their children to revise for exams.)*
11:30	iPod Hour *because* listening to classical music enhances the ability to focus and sustain attention. *(It also drowns the sound of sobbing chess LOSERS.)*
12:30	Lunch: tuna, wholegrain rice and green leafy vegetables *because* (see Breakfast above). *(Fish is the food of the devil. And sharks. No wonder they're so aggressive.)*
13:30	Building Mental Muscle Hour *because* keeping your brain cells active prevents deterioration. *(Er, brains don't contain muscles.)*
14:30	Positive Thinking Hour *because* positive thoughts rewire your, brain, strengthening the areas that stimulate positive feelings. *(Whatever.)*

15:30	Double Science Hour *because* teaching by observation, evidence collection and analysis, science helps sharpen your thinking about everyday ideas and events. *(But you're not allowed to 'chit-chat'.)*
17:30	Tea: trout and green leafy vegetables *because* (see Breakfast above). *(Curses on fish and green leafy vegetables.)*
18:30	Reading Hour *(Too busy burping up trout to read.)*
19:30	Three-minute phonecall to parent or guardian. *(Possibly more enjoyable for students whose mothers remove their earphones and speak to them.)*
20:30	Bedtime.

18

Guinea Pigs

"What is *this*?" Ms Grimm stands in front of my bed, holding my defaced LOSERS' routine between her thumb and forefinger as if it might carry something contagious. Uh-oh.

The other girls flee the dorm to begin morning exercises.

"It's my, um, routine sheet."

"Your 'um routine sheet'?"

I nod, my body tense.

"Think you're a comedian, Hawkins?" Ms Grimm asks.

I hate questions with no good answers. "Not sure."

"You think this is funny?" Ms Grimm reads from the sheet in a voice that would kill any joke. "'Run up and down stairs five times because exercise enhances brain function by increasing blood flow to the brain . . . *if it doesn't kill you first.*' Is that funny?"

"No." Not any more. "Sorry."

"You will be. If you don't want to run up and down the stairs five times, let's see how you feel about doing it twenty times."

"Twenty?" She must be joking.

I look at her face. She's not joking. Twenty trips up those huge staircases? On these puny legs?

The first trip up and down isn't too bad, but then everything blurs into a long run of "Owww!" and "I-can't-breathe!"

Somewhere around the fourteenth run up and down, I have to swerve to avoid a girl who staggers out of a room on the top floor. A woman in a nurse's uniform grabs her and drags her back into the room. The girl doesn't look like a LOSERS' student. Her hair's all over the place and she's wearing pyjamas in the middle of the day.

I wonder for a moment if she might have been a clue, but decide she's just a sick person in need of a good hairbrush. Either that or an illusion caused by too much exercise.

"Stop!" Ms Grimm barks from the bottom of the stairwell five minutes later.

"Willingly." I collapse, wheezing.

Wild

Wild

Fuzzy Hair

Pyjamas

(in the daytime?)

"The Great Leader has requested an audience with you, later this week." Ms Grimm is breathing heavily. I don't know why. It's not like *she's* been pounding up and down the stairs. "You are a lucky, lucky girl. Such a wonderful man."

A man? So Ms Grimm isn't the Great Leader. I look at her closely. Is she dribbling? The pupils of her eyes are huge and her face is sweaty. I flick through the unusual facial expressions stored in my memory and decide she's over-excited.

During breakfast, I'm so busy trying to picture a man who could make Ms Grimm dribble that I accidentally eat a herring. As the salty tail brushes my tonsils, yesterday's fish reappear in my throat and it's a struggle not to empty my stomach all over the dining table.

I can still taste herring in Chess Hour. I let Remarkable Student Aisha win because I can't bear the thought of her crying through Maths Hour when I feel this sick. The sickness fades slightly when Ms Grimm announces we're having double Maths instead of Music. After yesterday's scree-chathon, violins have shot up to second place (below fish) in my list of Things I Hate Most in the Whole World.

Ms Grimm hands out turquoise iPods during today's maths test. I immediately think of Mum's Curry in a Hurry freebie.

CLUE 21

The colour turquoise connects LOSERS,
Curry in a Hurry, Kazinsky Electronics,
the cab driver and now these iPods.

I put in the earphones. The music helps me focus and the test answers come easily as I whizz through the paper. Behind me, one Remarkable Student rushes out of the room with a nosebleed and another complains of a headache and has to be taken to the nurse.

Is this what people mean by exam nerves? For *Fermat's* sake, it's only a maths test.

We return the iPods and mark our own papers under the watchful eye of Mr Kumar (Maths Teacher). I can't stop staring at him.

CLUE 22

Mr Kumar (maths teacher) is the spitting image of Curry in a Hurry Man.

I think they have the same surname too. I was going to add that to my clue list until Remarkable Student Sandeep told me that over forty million people in India have the name Kumar. It didn't seem such a good clue after that.

I glance up in surprise as Mr Kumar hands me a shiny new iPod.

"Every student whose test score has increased by more than five per cent since yesterday gets their own personal media player," he explains.

Nice! The only downside is they have Ms Grimm's face engraved on the back. The iPods, that is, not the high-performing students. Engraving students would be child abuse.

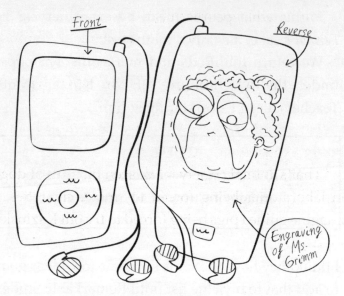

Front

Reverse

Engraving of Ms. Grimm

"Expensive reward," I mutter.

"Probably discounted." Porter appears behind me. "Mr Kazinsky, the science teacher, owns a big electronics store in town."

"Mr Kazinsky? Of Kazinsky Electronics? Teaches here?"

I'm pretty sure there aren't forty million Kazinskys in the world. More links. More connections. How wide has Ms Grimm cast her net?

"Why would someone with a successful electronics business want to be a science teacher?"

"No idea." Porter scratches his mother's face off the back of the iPod. "But I heard him thank Mother for finding such perfect guinea pigs."

"He's paid in guinea pigs?"

Porter rolls his eyes. The movement reminds me of Holly and I realise this is the first time we've gone more than forty-eight hours without speaking.

"He meant guinea pigs to test his products on," Porter explains.

"That's animal cruelty." I've seen pictures of dogs in laboratories being forced to smoke cigarettes. I imagine guinea pigs being forced to try out Kazinsky sandwich makers and hair straighteners. "We should report him."

Porter's expression makes him look even more like my sister. "He wasn't talking about *real* guinea pigs. Mother hates animals – have you seen any round here?"

"Only the other Remarkable Students." I stop laughing when I see Porter's face.

CLUE 23
Porter thinks Mr Kazinsky and Ms Grimm
are testing electronic devices on LOSERS.

That's worse than testing them on animals. Unless you're an animal. I should tell the police. This might be connected to Dad's disappearance. They want to test products on clever people – Dad is a very clever person.

I have a new theory. Well, a new, improved theory.

> **(RECAP)**
> **THEORY A**
> **SOMEONE HAS KIDNAPPED DAD**

+

(RECAP)
CLUE 10
The Kazinsky Electronics van is parked outside our house almost every day now.

+

(RECAP)
CLUE 23
Porter thinks Mr Kazinsky and Ms Grimm are testing electronic devices on LOSERS.

=

THEORY B
MS GRIMM KIDNAPPED DAD TO USE
HIM AS THE PERFECT GUINEA PIG
FOR MR KAZINSKY'S PRODUCTS.

I open my mouth to interrogate Porter but Ms Grimm swoops down and whisks him away.

19

Cleverness

I grab the seat next to Porter in Building Mental Muscle Hour and poke him with my pencil. Ms Grimm glares at me. I give her an apologetic smile and kick her son under the table.

"Talk to me," I hiss. "What's going on with this place? Why did you bring me here last week? Why was the taxi driver wearing a turquoise bracelet? And why didn't you want your mother to know we'd met?"

"Not now," Porter murmurs from the side of his mouth as Ms Grimm bangs her ruler on the desk and scans the room for someone to yell at.

"Just answer three simple questions." I scribble on his paper:

1) Where's my dad?

2) Was the taxi driver a plant?

3) What are you hiding from your mother?

He scribbles underneath, next to a doodle of a portaloo:

1) No idea

2) Yes

3) Not a simple question

Now stop it! Mother's watching.

So I've learnt one thing:

CLUE 24

The taxi driver was a plant, waiting to
pick us up and bring us to LOSERS.

Does this mean some of my clues aren't clues at all? I need to talk to Holly. I hadn't realised how much my conversations with her help me figure things out.

Ms Grimm raps her stick against the board. "Today, we're discussing candidates for Cleverest Person in the World. I'll begin by nominating James

Watson, who co-discovered the DNA double helix structure and believed biotechnology could cure stupidity."

My hyperactive brain recalls googling James Watson for a school project.

"He claimed biotechnology could cure ugliness too," I remember. "He said, 'People say it would be terrible if we made all girls pretty. I think it would be great!'"

The boys laugh, the girls scowl and Ms Grimm swaps her vote to Marie Curie. I slap my hand over my mouth to stop myself pointing out that since Marie Curie's been dead since 1934 she's probably not that clever any more.

Porter suggests Kate Beckinsale for World's Cleverest Person. He explains she's an actress who went to Oxford University but is mainly famous for being a hot vampire in the *Underworld* movies.

Ms Grimm switches off the Smart Board, snaps her stick and hands out worksheets. But she doesn't make Porter run up and down the stairs twenty times. Teacher's pet.

I stare out the window. We're on the top floor and I have an almost aerial view of the surroundings.

Then it hits me. I've seen this pattern before.

To the left is the large square outline of the castle walls. In the far left corner are the turrets of the castle. Behind me are Mum's favourite shoe shops. I reach into my pocket for the copy of the map I've been carrying around for two months. Finally, it makes sense:

I peer at the arrows with black circles inside. I have a horrible suspicion someone was trying to draw aerial views of giant high heels.

X marks the spot.

CLUE 25

The ugly picture was guiding me to LOSERS.

But why? Who sent it? And what "treasure" is marked by that red cross? The more I think about Theory B (Someone has kidnapped Dad to use him as the perfect guinea pig) the harder it is to believe LOSERS would go to all this trouble just to test electronic products.

Another theory is forming, based on James Watson's claims. The ones about intelligence, that is. Not the ones about pretty girls. I don't think pretty girls are relevant to this case.

Dad was convinced it was possible to make people smarter. Ms Grimm must agree or she wouldn't have made LOSERS' mission statement: "To increase the intelligence of bright young people". That's what she's trying to achieve with the fish dinners, turquoise walls and motivational quotes. But what if they're not working fast enough for her?

CLUE 26
Dad, who is one of the world's top brain scientists, was last seen outside an institute dedicated to increasing intelligence.

I have a new theory.

+

+

=

THEORY C
MS GRIMM KIDNAPPED DAD
TO FORCE HIM TO DEVELOP
INTELLIGENCE-IMPROVING DEVICES.

125

Wait! I forgot CLUE 24 – the taxi driver was a plant. Does that mean we can't trust anything he said? Is CLUE 26 no longer a clue? Was Dad dropped off at LOSERS or not? And what does this mean for THEORY C?

Argh. My head hurts. I really need to talk to Holly. Instead I have to go to Positive Thinking Hour. Ironic, considering my thoughts are mainly about kidnapping and fish dinners, and are entirely negative.

20

Mental Conditioning

I march to the front of the classroom, determined to confront Ms Grimm while everyone's filling in their worksheets. But by the time I get there I've lost my nerve and I just mumble, "Er, Ms Grimm, have you met my dad?"

"Met him?" Ms Grimm raises a hand to her chest and flutters her sparse eyelashes. "Yes, indeed. We were at Oxford University together."

"With Kate Beckinsale, the hot vampire?"

Ms Grimm continues as if I haven't spoken. "I've followed his career closely ever since."

CLUE 27

Ms Grimm knows Dad and is clearly a fan.

"He's a great thinker," she adds. "One of a kind. Although he believed you could follow in his footsteps."

"He did?"

"Yes. I planned to discuss this with you yesterday but I was distracted by your observations on my LOSERS routine. On reflection, I realise you were merely exercising your superior intelligence."

"I was?"

Ms Grimm nods. "Sometimes it's difficult for those as intelligent as you or I to remain entirely positive. Luckily, my Mental Conditioning Room can help with that."

"Your what?"

Ms Grimm asks Mr Kumar (maths) to watch the class and holds the door open. "Come! I'll show you."

I follow her, hoping she'll tell me more about Dad.

"Mental conditioning?" I process the words. "Isn't that another way of saying brainwashing?"

"Would that be so bad?" Ms Grimm strides down the long, turquoise corridor. "If you ask me, most people's brains would benefit from a good wash." She turns another corner and pushes open a heavy wooden door. "Here we are, Hawkins. Welcome to my Mental Conditioning Room."

I expect a scary white laboratory full of screaming student guinea pigs wired to machines. Instead, I find a cosy library with floor to ceiling shelves overflowing with books and magazines. The latest scientific journals are piled on a round wooden table in the middle of the room and in each corner is a black leather reclining chair with turquoise earphones attached. A large silver mirror on the back wall reflects everything, making the room look bigger than it is.

Ms Grimm pushes me down into one of the black chairs. "This is where we help our most advanced students develop their abilities. All you have to do is put in these earphones."

I fight the urge to shove her away. I like it better when she's being nasty. At least you know where you stand. It's a relief when a mobile phone alarm goes off in the corridor and her creepy smile vanishes.

Mobile phones are strictly forbidden. You'd think if one of the "brightest young people in the country" managed to smuggle one inside then they'd have the sense not to set the alarm. Is someone looking for trouble?

Screeching in indignation, Ms Grimm flies to the door, pausing long enough to bark, "I'll only be a minute."

A minute is probably all she needs to assassinate the rule-breaker. I wipe the sweat from my forehead and breathe more easily. Every step towards the phone-offender is a step away from me.

My relief fades when Porter sprints past the doorway brandishing a mobile phone. What's he doing? His mother is clearly wondering the same thing.

"Porter Brian Grimm!" Ms Grimm powers down the corridor behind him, "Come back here, this minute!"

Ms Grimm's fast, but Porter's faster. She yells for backup. A man in thick glasses and slightly-too-short trousers bursts out of the room next door and chases after them, a heavy key chain jangling against his leg.

With the action taking off in the other direction, I sink back into the nearest leather recliner and stare at myself in the mirror. Is this the me I'd have seen a month ago? Dad gave me an article once, about Heraclitus' theory of flux, which suggested everything is in a state of constant change. But how much can you change before you become a completely different person? Four weeks ago I'd have disapproved of Porter breaking the rules. Today I want to cheer him on. (Quietly.)

As I gaze at my reflection I notice the mirror is set into the wall. Moving closer, it looks like the glass is glowing from the inside, as if lit from behind. I knock on the surface. Sounds hollow. Could this be one of those two-way mirrors you get on TV detective shows? I cup my hands around my eyes and press my face close to the glass. I can't be sure but I think I see something behind it. A TV? No, a computer screen. And what's that in the corner?

Trying not to imagine what Ms Grimm will do to me if she discovers I ignored her instructions, I creep into the corridor, glancing left and right to make sure no one's looking. If that is a two-way mirror, the spy room must be the next door along – the door Short Trousers Jangly Keys Guy didn't have time to lock behind him.

Something sinister is going on at LOSERS and I'm sure it's connected to Dad's disappearance. This room might hold the secrets.

Then again, it might just hold a big heap of trouble. What to do?

Holly would barge straight in. Month-Ago-Me would stay put and wait for Ms Grimm to return. Today-Me stands half in, half out the room, unable to make a decision.

Porter comes flying around the corner and skids to a halt, three doors down. He jams the handle up and down, smashing his shoulder against the door and swearing when it refuses to open. You'd think it was a roomful of portaloos the way he's behaving.

I move across to join him. "What's in there?"

"Answers." Porter kicks the door.

I thought Porter *had* the answers. Well, most of them at least. Maybe we can find the rest together.

"This door's not locked." I point behind me. "Want to check it out?"

Porter looks at the door and then at his watch. "They'll be here any second. I'll distract them for another five minutes while you slip inside. But you have to tell me what you find. Promise?"

I nod.

He takes a deep breath and releases it in a mad whoop before running off down the corridor.

21

Spying

I'm committed now. I promised Porter. Closing my eyes, I fling myself into the room.

Albert Einstein! I was right. I'm on the spy side of a two-way mirror. Next to the glass are two wooden, fold-up chairs. One is still warm. My eyes lock on to the device in the far corner of the room pointing directly at the chair I was sitting in only minutes ago. I approach it slowly, reaching out to touch the turquoise plastic to convince myself it's real.

CLUE 28
LOSERS have created a life-
size model of the brain ray!

It matches our design in almost every way. The only differences are:

1. The disgusting turquoise colour.
2. The +/- dial on the side. That wasn't part of our design. Positive and negative what?

I jump as something beeps behind me, then laugh shakily when I see it's just the computer I spotted from the other side of the glass. I must have nudged the monitor and brought it to life.

On the screen is a list of folders, filed alphabetically:

- *West, Alexander*
- Winston, Robert
- Wittgenstein, Ludwig
- Wright, Wilbur & Orville
- Xenocrates
- Young, Grace Chisholm

The names in regular font are famous scientists and mathematicians. I click on Robert Winston and find his folder full of speeches he's made and articles he's written. One of the italic names is familiar too.

Alexander West is a fellow Remarkable Student. Maybe we all have student folders. Curious, I hit the arrow key and scroll up to "H".

- Galileo
- *Gold, Gemma*
- *Grimm, Porter*
- Hawking, Stephen
- Hawkins, Brian
- Hawkins, Madeleine
- *Hawkins, Noelle*

There I am. I insert my memory stick and copy the file.

I recognise Gemma Gold's name too – the girl who forgot her comfort blanket.

It's not a big surprise to find Dad on the list. He's a well-known figure – the wacky scientist TV people call when they want to make their programme more controversial. But then I register the name between Dad's and mine – "Hawkins, Madeleine".

Mum?

Mum has never written a book or appeared in a television documentary. Mum's not a scientist. This makes no sense.

CLUE 29

LOSERS are interested in my mum.

I try to stop my hand shaking so I can select Mum's folder, but just as I'm about to copy it I glance at the two-way mirror and see the door to the Mental Conditioning Room swing open.

Isaac Newton! Ms Grimm is back!

I check the clock at the bottom of the computer screen. Seven minutes have passed. Porter kept his side of the bargain. I'm the one who messed up. And Ms Grimm is going to mentally condition me to death as a result.

I whip out the memory stick without following the proper ejection procedures and run as fast as my PE-hating legs will carry me. Halfway down the corridor, I see Short Trousers Jangly Keys Guy heading my way and dart into the girls' toilets.

Toilets! Brilliant! The perfect excuse for not being in the Mental Conditioning Room. Everyone has to wee. After washing my hands to support my story, I leave the loo and head back towards Ms Grimm.

Perhaps today isn't my day to die. Hey, maybe that counts as a positive thought.

I seem to have got away with it. Ms Grimm only

stays in the Mental Conditioning Room long enough to tell me she can't stay in the Mental Conditioning Room.

"I need to deal with Porter," she snaps. "Wait here until the bell rings for Science Hour."

I want to find Porter and help him. It's partly my fault he's in trouble. But I'm convinced Short Trousers Jangly Keys Guy is on the other side of the mirror, so I flick through the science journals, giving the odd fake laugh as if I've spotted a particularly funny scientific anecdote, until the bell finally rings.

After that, I race to the Science Lab. Porter's not there either. Where is he? What's the Grimm Reaper doing to him?

I set up my combustion experiment and picture myself pointing the Bunsen burner at Mr Kazinsky, forcing him to reveal Porter's whereabouts. In my enthusiasm, I accidentally burn a hole in the workbench.

Mr Kazinsky confiscates the Bunsen burner, gazing into the flame with a strange, absorbed expression before handing me an electromagnetism worksheet. Considering I've only been at LOSERS for two days, I've spent a lot of time completing electromagnetism worksheets. Is this another coincidence?

137

The design sketches for the brain ray included notes on using electromagnetic energy to increase intelligence. Dad said we were on the verge of a huge discovery. And then he disappeared.

Did LOSERS build their brain ray using the plans Fake Insurance Man stole? Or have they tortured the details out of Dad?

I pick up the pen to fill in the electromagnetism worksheet. My hand shakes as I remember how I was tricked into calculating how to blow up a porta-loo-sized box. Just because I *can* work out how to do something, that doesn't necessarily mean I *should*. I put the lid back on my pen and refuse to complete the worksheet.

But it may be too late. What if Ms Grimm has already figured out how to use electromagnetic waves to alter IQ levels?

22

Breaking Rules

Mr Kumar announces Porter is unwell and won't be joining us for dinner. I'm desperate to leave the dining room and find him – partly to check he's okay, partly to keep my promise about updating him on the secret spy room, but mainly to escape yet another fish supper.

Tonight's fish has its head attached and the big, bulgy eye follows me all the way to top table, where Ms Grimm's gobbling up her dinner, bulgy eyes and all.

"I feel sick," I say truthfully. "Can I lie down in the dorm?"

Ms Grimm dribbles fish juice. I take that as a yes and I run from the dining room, gulping in non-fishy air. I find Porter lying on the sofa in the sitting room, reading a book called *Tracing Missing Persons*.

He drops it when he sees me. "So? What did you find?"

I describe the room behind the mirror with its still-warm chair, its computer files and its real-life brain ray. Porter listens closely, nodding as if it all makes perfect sense. His head shoots up when I mention Gemma Gold.

"Did you get copies of the files?"

I pull my memory stick out my pocket and confess, "Only my own. *Fibonacci!* I should have copied yours too, shouldn't I? Especially when you were the one doing the risky stuff. Sorry, Porter, I wasn't thinking and then I ran out of time."

"Don't worry. It wasn't *my* file I wanted. And there was no risk. My mother wouldn't hurt me. I can't believe she took my phone."

"I can't believe she let you keep it in the first place. I've seen how seriously they take the no-phone rule here. No mobiles. No internet access. Only one call home a day and you have to have a teacher in the room."

CLUE 30

LOSERS are obsessed with blocking
our access to the outside world.

"Mother trusts . . . trusted me." Porter squeezes the sofa cushion until his knuckles turn white. "And I trusted her. Also past tense. I can't believe she took my phone."

"If it's so important to you, why were you waving it about in front of her?"

"I was creating a distraction. I saw Mother take you into the Mental Conditioning Room and I didn't want her to plug you into anything. There's something wrong with that room. A few kids come out super-bright. Others not so much . . ."

"What do you mean?"

Porter glances over his shoulder, even though we're the only people in the room. "I've said too much already."

"You haven't said anything," I protest. "And you know what's going on around here, don't you?"

"I thought I did." Porter frowns. "I thought this was a money-making scam where Mother got geeks – no offence – to do complicated calculations for big businesses and try out new products for weirdos like Kazinsky. But there's something else going on. Something no one's talking about. Something that makes people vanish."

"Do you mean Dad?"

"Among others." Porter scans the room, checking the exits. "We should listen to your file, Noelle. Who

141

knows how long we've got before they come for us?"

"But you haven't explained . . ." I pause as the recording starts.

"Don't let others drag you down. It's not enough to have a good mind. The important thing is to use it. Nobody remembers who came in second. The first man gets the oyster; the second man gets the shell . . .

Whoa. This sounds familiar. I can see Porter recognises it too. The recording in the in LOSERS' brainwashing file matches the one in Dad's shoes.

I yank out the memory stick, failing to follow the correct removal procedures for the second time today. I'm turning into a cyber-rebel.

"Talking shoes and two-way mirrors?" Porter frowns. "Meals aren't the only fishy things around here. I don't understand half of what's going on any more."

"If it makes you feel better, I don't understand *any* of what's going on."

It doesn't make Porter feel better because he's not listening.

He pauses, halfway through the door. "Remember that locked room I wanted to get into earlier?"

I nod.

"It's full of screens showing CCTV footage from secret cameras they've set up here and in other places around town. If we can get in, we'll find out more about what's going on. You up for it?"

"You are joking? You're already in trouble for the mobile phone thing. Wait . . . Did you say CCTV footage?"

"Yup." Porter keeps walking, forcing me to jog down the corridor behind him. "Come on. Best time to break a rule is straight after you've been punished for breaking the last one. No one suspects you're still up to no good."

It sounds logical, but the glint in Porter's eye makes me nervous. I consider the possibility that he's gone completely mad.

"Besides," he adds, "you want to see the CCTV footage."

"No, *you* want to see the CCTV footage."

But Porter's right. I do want to see it – because I haven't forgotten CLUE 17:

(RECAP)
CLUE 17
Someone has installed CCTV
cameras around our home.

23

Spy Cameras

Porter slows to a halt outside the CCTV Room. He tries the handle.

"Still locked?" I'm torn between relief and disappointment.

"Don't worry. I made a deal with the IT bloke while he was 'keeping an eye' on me earlier."

"Short Trousers Jangly Keys Guy?"

"I call him Dave." Porter knocks on the CCTV room door.

The door creaks open and an arm shoots out, pulling us into a small, dimly lit room that looks just how I've always imagined the New Scotland Yard CCTV room must look. A heavy desk runs the entire length of one wall. Above it are rows of box-shaped shelves. Each gap contains a laptop, creating a wall of monitors. I count quickly – ten along, two up: twenty in all. A mirror on the opposite wall gives the impression the screens go on forever.

"Oi! What's *she* doing here?" Jangly Keys Dave hisses when he spots me. "Flaming Nora. As if one of you wasn't bad enough."

"Relax," Porter says while I wonder if Flaming Nora is a famous mathematician.

Jangly Keys Dave doesn't relax. "You've got five minutes." He snatches Porter's laptop and flounces out the door.

"Ignore Dave," Porter says. "He's a bit touchy but

he's agreed to open locked doors if I let him use my laptop."

"Huh? The place is full of laptops."

"Yes, but mine has internet connection."

I gape at Porter.

Porter grins. "It's also the only computer in this building that's not being monitored."

"How do you know that?" I ask.

"Because Dave's in charge of monitoring it."

Porter's grin fades and he reaches for two of the CCTV room laptops laptops and turns their screens towards me.

"Is this why you were interested in the footage?"

Archimedes! Images of home flicker in front of me.

CLUE 31
It was LOSERS who installed spy
cameras to monitor my family.

I gaze at the laptop screens in disbelief. Each screen is split into four smaller windows. One laptop shows images from inside my house, the other shows images from outside. Holly is standing in the top-left square of the indoors laptop. As I watch her gaze out through our living-room window, I get a sharp pain in my stomach. Must be the herrings.

Holly's spiky hand movements suggest she's arguing with someone outside. I check the other laptop and see Smokin' Joe and the Toilet Trolls swaggering up the garden path. I turn up the volume. I shouldn't have bothered; all I hear are nasty jokes about Mum's weight.

"Who are those idiots?" Porter asks.

I give him a brief history of my life with Smokin' Joe. He brightens up when I mention the Toilet Trolls until I explain they hang out in traditional toilets rather than portable ones. When I get to the part about being dumped in the wheelie bin, Porter grabs the microphone beside the laptop and presses the on switch.

His voice thunders through the speakers, distorted and robotic.

"Smokin' Joe Slater," Porter booms. "This is your God speaking."

Smokin' Joe looks up at the sky, clutching his chest.

"Leave the Hawkins family alone," God/Porter orders. "Or I shall be forced to smite you."

Smokin' Joe mutters something to the Toilet Trolls, who shrug and screw up their faces.

I put my hand over the microphone. "I don't think they understand 'smite'."

Porter frowns. "Hello! God again. Just to be clear,

I'm saying if you continue to bully the Hawkins family I will strike you down with a massive bolt of godly lightning." Porter pauses and adds, "Like Thor. From *The Avengers*."

That works. The Toilet Trolls grab each other for support and Smokin' Joe cowers behind the hedge.

I grab the mic. "And then I'll give you a wedgie."

Although the microphone alters my voice, it's still higher pitched than Porter's. Fortunately, no one seems to notice.

Porter mouths, "Not very godlike."

But I'm on a roll. "And if you don't get away from my house, I'll remind everyone about the time you wet your pants in Year Three."

The Toilet Trolls snigger. Smokin' Joe punches the nearest one and storms off down the street.

Porter mouths, "*My* house?"

Oops.

"When I say *my* house, I obviously mean in the sense that *all* houses are my house. Because I am God. Of everything. Especially houses."

The Toilet Trolls are too busy pushing and shoving each other to notice the slip-up. But in the top corner of the indoors laptop, Holly's jaw drops open and she stumbles backwards, hitting the sofa. The force of her momentum carries her over the back of the couch and on to Mum's stomach, which bounces her back on to her feet.

Porter slides off his chair, spluttering with laughter.

"Know-All?" Holly straightens her top, trying to act like nothing happened. "Is that you?"

Outside in the corridor, footsteps are thudding towards the CCTV room. Our five minutes are up. I grab the mic.

"Yes. Quick, Holly! I need to talk to you—"

The door bangs open behind me.

"Run, Holly. Go to the comput—"

24

Missing Girl

Jangly Keys Dave snatches the microphone. "What do you think you're doing? Ms Grimm watches these recordings."

The colour drains from Porter's face.

"Don't worry," I reassure him. "You're still alive. She can't know you've been sneaking out."

Some of Porter's colour returns.

"There must be lots of things Dave doesn't show her."

Little blobs of red appear on Dave's cheeks. "I don't like giving her bad news. She gets a little . . . excited."

"Yeah. I can imagine." Porter sits up. "So can we agree this won't appear in your highlights reel?"

"I'll go one better and edit it out altogether. You're not the only ones who'll suffer if she sees it." Dave plugs in his earphones and scans the footage in reverse. "Blimey. Does that girl ever sit still?"

He plays it forwards and we watch at high speed as Holly tries to get through the front door disguised as a dog, a rat, a potted plant and a large cockroach. I'm particularly impressed by her attempt to scuttle out beneath the folds of Vigil-Aunty's vintage fox-fur coat. I've never been convinced that old fox died before it became a piece of clothing, so it's good to see Holly emerge unbitten. She doesn't make it through the door though. Vigil-Aunty fishes her out and deposits her back in the living room.

Dave shakes his head, presses a few buttons and scans forward to real time as Holly heads up to my room, presumably to use the computer.

He thrusts Porter's laptop at us and sticks his earphones back in. "Done. Now clear off."

"Distract him for five minutes," I hiss at Porter. "Get him away from that computer."

Porter tugs at Dave's earphones and pulls him across to look at another laptop, where Remarkable Student Aisha is punishment-jogging up and down the stairs. I hope it's not because of our conversation.

Scowling at Dave's laughter, I rub my leg muscles, still sore from my own punishment-jog, and vow Aisha will not suffer in vain.

One eye on Dave, I switch on the indoor laptop's webcam and point it at the mirror. The webcam will now capture all the footage reflected in the mirror – from our front room, my bedroom, my parents' bedroom and the entrance hall. All I have to do is make a call to Porter's laptop and send the images from the webcam to his screen. Then I'll be able to see everything that's happening at home on Porter's laptop, wherever I am in the building.

Perfect. "Time to go!" I announce.

"Too right!" Dave tears his attention away from Aisha and bundles us out the door, locking it behind us.

I head for Reading Hour with Porter's laptop clasped beneath my arm.

Porter veers left.

"Where are you going?" I ask him.

"Out. Digging for gold," he says with a twisted smile.

"Wait for me. I'll come with you. I want to talk to Holly."

He shakes his head. "The receptionist will call Mother if we leave together, but she's used to me popping out after school to check on new portaloo displays. Better if you stay here and cover for me. I'll pop in on Holly if you want."

"But she won't . . . Wait . . ."

Too late. Porter slips through the front door before I can warn him that he might not get a very friendly greeting from my sister.

I feel lost. Even though I'm not sure I can trust him, Porter is the closest thing I've got to a friend in here.

No one looks up when I walk into Reading Hour. They're all either plugged into their iPods or fussing over Remarkable Student Aisha, whose nose is bleeding. Must be all that running. I keep telling people exercise is dangerous.

It's weird. I'd never seen anyone have a nosebleed before Mum had hers last month, but now they're happening all over the place. I try to convince myself it's just a coincidence and my brain is fooling itself into creating patterns where they don't exist. But I can't escape the feeling that everything is somehow connected.

I glance around the room and spot a quiet corner out of camera range and half hidden by a fake pot plant. I don't turn on my iPod, but I slip in my earphones. Easier to blend in when you act like everyone else.

I flip open Porter's laptop and watch Holly stumble through the Meccano solar system to get to my computer.

Noelle Hawkins: *Holly! Itz me. Tlk n txtspk.*
Sm1 cd b watchn

Holly Hawkins: *NoL? C%l! HRU?*

Noelle Hawkins: *Gd. Woch ot – LSRs cn c u &*
heA u & c yr emsgs

Holly Hawkins: *ru sAyn they set ^ d cams?*

Noelle Hawkins: *Yes. Trst n01. BTW Porter iz*
comin 2 c u

Holly Hawkins: *Rly? Cnt BLEv he lied bout*
LSRs N bn d son of d TGR! Wot
a :@)

Noelle Hawkins: ...

I'm halfway through replying that Porter's not 'rly' a
':@)' when the Grimm Reaper walks into iPod hour.
I stuff the laptop into the pot plant and pretend to be
listening to my iPod. For the next fifteen minutes I
put all my energy into looking innocent.

When Ms Grimm is distracted by yet another
student nosebleed, I risk a glance through the
fake foliage at the CCTV images on the laptop
screen.

Fibonacci! Fake Insurance Man is back at the house
with Ug and Thug. I watch in horror as Ug grabs

Holly, who wriggles like a hyperactive worm and makes a dive for the chainsaw.

Too slow.

Thug whips the chainsaw from her grip and whirls it dangerously close to her head. Nasty. You don't want to be hit by a chainsaw, even if it's switched off. As Holly tries to break free, Thug carries the tool out of the room.

Why does Holly have to fight everyone? She's going to get hurt and I'm not there to help or at least to call for someone else to help! I'm clutching the tops of my arms so tightly I cut the skin with my nails. I try to relax my grip but it's hard when Ug has Holly in a headlock.

Thug is back. He heads across to the window. What's he doing? No. NO. NO! Not my computer. *Archimedes!* There goes the hard drive. And one, two, three, four, five, six monitors. They must know we've been in contact.

They'll be coming for me next.

25

Interrogation

Ms Grimm doesn't look at me as she leaves the room. Is that a good sign? Or is she lulling me into a false sense of security before slicing me into tiny pieces? Where is Porter? Does he know about the raid on my house? Can I trust him?

My fingers hover over the laptop keyboard and before I can stop myself I hit alt + tab. Porter's Hotmail page pops up, email address entered, just waiting for the password.

Hacking is a criminal offence and Porter is a (sort of) friend, but he did admit he planted the taxi at the Valentine's market and he still hasn't explained why.

I glance around guiltily and type: P-o-r-t-e-r-1.

Ping. *That password is incorrect. Try again.*

That's probably a sign I should respect Porter's privacy, but I can't stop my brain flicking through the password-relevant things I know about him. Dad says guessing other people's passwords is all about getting inside their heads.

I've been inside Porter's brain: I've watched his portaloo movie.

Slowly, carefully, I type: s-p-l-e-n-d-a-m-i-n-i-3-0-0-0

And I'm in. It's that easy.

I skim Porter's inbox. There are a lot of communications with portaloo companies. Between these are a few messages from your_great_leader@ yahoo.com. I feel better about hacking into Porter's account when I spot one titled, USE PORTALOO EXPLOSION FOOTAGE TO GET NOELLE HAWKINS TO LINDON.

Ada Lovelace! The Great Leader and Porter are plotting against me. I hadn't realised how much I wanted to trust Porter until now, when I find out I can't.

I skim the email but it just gives my address and the cab driver's number. Nothing about why the Great Leader wants me here or what happened to Dad.

The other messages from your_great_leader@ yahoo.com are group emails to All Remarkable Students. I read the most recent:

You are the brightest and the best.
You can shine brighter than the rest.
That is our quest.
Await our call.

The poem is so bad it's almost funny, but I can't laugh at the idea of a legion of ex-LOSERS awaiting their call to action:

CLUE 32

The Great Leader of LOSERS is
creating an army-in-waiting.

A physically feeble army, perhaps, but an army with brains.

They have to be stopped. But who's going to stop them? I can't trust Porter, I can no longer contact Holly and Ms Grimm could be coming for me at any minute.

There's only one solution – escape! If Porter can leave LOSERS so can I. I've already worked out how. Our ground-floor dorm backs on to the alleyway where the bins are stored. All the windows have child-proof locks "for student safety", but someone has fiddled with the lock on my cubicle window so it opens. I like to think this is a sign Gemma Gold arranged her own disappearance – although every time I look at the tatty comfort blanket I get a bad feeling.

I still have the cameras to worry about, but if I leave when the Grimm Reaper is busy, I'm confident it'll be hours before Jangly Keys Dave builds up enough courage to tell her I've gone. I stroke the calculator money in my pocket. I should be far away by then.

Home!

I ask the cabbie to stop at the end of our street so I can avoid the CCTV cameras. I clamber through the neighbours' back gardens like a trainee burglar and realise my stealth tactics need work when Mrs Burnett at number 31 gives me a cheery wave.

Finally I'm in my own backyard. I gaze up at Holly's window. *Descartes!* How did Porter get up there?

Drainpipe vs oak tree? I choose oak. Ow! Spiky branch. Twig in my eye. Twig. In. My. Eye.

I'm ready to give up altogether until I hear Porter's voice coming from the window above me. Gritting my teeth and closing my twig-eye, I scramble faster, ripping my shirt and scraping the flesh of my arms.

But by the time I reach the window, Holly has

Porter in a stranglehold and is forcing him down onto her pink swivel chair. Before I can say, "I was worrying about the wrong person," Porter is strapped to the seat with Holly's bedside lamp shining in his eyes.

Holly beams when she spots me. "Know-All? Brilliant! Wasn't expecting you!"

Porter struggles against the dressing-gown belt that's holding his hands in place. "Noelle! Thank God! Tell your sister to untie me!"

Wary of the gleam in Holly's eyes, I speak softly. "Um, Holly, don't you think this might be a little extreme?"

Holly shakes her head. "He needs convincing to tell us the truth."

"There's 'convincing' and then there's human rights abuse."

But I do nothing to release Porter. There are several reasons for this:

     i. I don't want Holly to attack me instead
     ii. I'm curious to see what she does next
     iii. Holly's right – Porter does need convincing to tell us the truth

Holly waggles the lamp at him. "You WILL tell us what's going on."

"I'm telling you nothing until you release me."

"We'll see about that." Holly stalks from the room.

"Untie me. Quick," Porter begs. "Before she comes back."

"She's bigger than I am," I protest weakly.

"Not by much."

"Yeah, but she's way scarier."

"True," Porter agrees. "What if I tell you whatever it is she wants to know? Do you think she'll let me go?

"Worth a try. You can start by telling me why you contacted us in the first place."

Porter looks at the floor. "Someone told me to."

"The Great Leader?"

Before Porter has a chance to respond, Holly returns with a pint of water and pours it over his head.

"Water torture," she declares. "Ha! What do you say now?"

Porter shakes his head in disbelief. "I say you don't know much about water torture."

Holly glares at him.

"He has a point," I add. "He was talking before you came back. Now he's just dripping all over the carpet."

Holly's not convinced. "I'm going to get something that'll really make him talk," she says, stomping from the room.

"Hurry up. Tell me everything," I urge Porter. "Who knows what she'll come back with?"

Porter talks fast. "The Great Leader told me to show you the exploding toilet footage to lure you to Lindon. After that, the driver's orders were to drive you to LOSERS and make you think you'd figured it out yourself."

"But why?"

"He didn't explain."

"I know, I saw the email. What I meant was why did you agree? Why trick us like that?"

"He said he'd help me find—" Porter stops and frowns. "What do you mean you saw the email?"

"I, uh, accessed your email account. Sorry."

"You read my emails?"

"No need to yell."

"NO NEED TO YELL?" Porter yells. "I'LL YELL IF I—"

G R R R R R R R R R R R R - G - G - G - G - GRRRRRRRRRRRRRRRRRRRRRRRRRRRRR.

I put my head in my hands. "I thought Thug and Ug took the chainsaw away with them. *Professor Brian Cox!* Why would they take the computer but leave the chainsaw?"

"Chainsaw?" The blood vanishes from Porter's face. "Your sister has a *chainsaw*?"

I don't need to reply, because Holly picks that

minute to stride into the room, revving her power tool.

Porter struggles to his feet and bounces across the room to the open window, still tied to the pink chair. He closes his eyes.

"Wait!" I dive for him, but I'm too slow.

Porter's gone. Out of the window. Chair and all.

Albert Einstein! He could have broken his legs – or worse. I can't even check he's okay because I'm scared of being sliced in half by a low-flying chainsaw. Holly is like a Rottweiler that's lost its favourite chew toy. A Rottweiler with a lethal weapon, which she brandishes out of the window, accidentally sawing her curtains in half.

"Enough!" I screech. "Turn that stupid thing off before you kill one of us."

Holly does as I say, for once. Her arms are shaking with the effort of holding the huge saw.

"Did you see him jump?" she asks. "Mental! There's no sign of him in the garden, so he must have made it. Wow!" She bends to pick up the curtain material from the floor. "Oops."

"'Oops'? That's all you have to say? You turn into a chainsaw-wielding crazy person and all you can say is 'Oops'? I suppose I should be glad there's no sign of Porter. It means he can still walk."

"Or roll," Holly giggles.

I scowl.

"Okay, okay, the chainsaw may have been a bit much," Holly admits as she ties the two halves of her curtains together.

"You think?"

"Anyway," Holly says, the near-chainsaw-massacre forgotten, "We need to get you back to that school, fast."

"But—"

"No buts. That's where Porter's headed. That's where the answers are. Do you want to find Dad or not?"

Holly doesn't play fair.

26

Bad Guys

"Pssst." I crouch in the alley, among fish bones and rotting vegetables, desperately trying to get Remarkable Student Aisha's attention so she can help me open my cubicle window.

I know she's in there but I daren't raise my head above the windowsill. It's almost eight-thirty (lights out) and Ms Grimm could be anywhere.

I pick up a broken beer bottle and tap the glass with it.

Finally Aisha appears at the window. "Stop it. You'll get us all in trouble. What are you doing out there?"

"No idle chit-chat," I remind her. "Open the window. Please?"

"I can't. I'll be punished."

"No one will notice if you just slide the window open a crack. But if you stand here arguing when

165

you're supposed to be getting ready for bed, someone's sure to notice and then you really will be in trouble."

Sighing miserably, Aisha pushes up the window and retreats rapidly to the other side of the dorm.

I launch myself through the window, hitting my head on the chest of drawers with a crunch. A small square of paper flutters out from behind the drawers.

Porter and Gemma? Porter told me he was "digging for gold". Was that Gold with a capital G? Is this the secret behind Porter's behaviour? I ignore my dorm mates' disapproving stares and head up the stairs to the boys' dorm to ask. But Porter's not back.

He's still not back two hours later.

He stuffed his bed before he left, so no one raised the alarm at lights out. He asked me to cover for him, but that was before he leapt out of the window. What if he's hurt and no one knows until it's too late?

I lie in bed, staring at the ceiling, imagining myself telling Ms Grimm he's gone. The thought sends a shiver down my spine. The shiver becomes a deep freeze when I hear a knock at the window. I don't know whose idea it was to put the girls' dorm on the ground floor, because despite the railings, the CCTV cameras and the patrolling teachers, we sometimes get unwanted visitors.

I peer over my bed covers, twisting so I can see into the cubicle, and cheer with relief when I see Porter's face at the window.

"Porter!" *Thank Fermat!*

He stands in the alley, making shushing signs from behind the glass.

I shush. The last thing I want to do is wake a sleeping mob of Remarkable Students. I open the window so Porter can slither through it. He lands headfirst in the bin.

"What are you doing?" I hiss.

"Making a grand entrance!" He flicks a banana skin off his shoulder. "Quick. Bathroom. No cameras there."

He hops through the dorm and into the bathroom. As he lowers himself onto the edge of the

167

bath tub, I notice his ankle is turning a nasty shade of purple.

"Hurts," he says miserably, when he sees me looking.

I wince in sympathy. "Sorry about Holly."

"Can't blame her for being angry." Porter grimaces as he stretches the leg out. "I shouldn't have tricked you."

"Did you decide that before or after Holly waved a chainsaw in your face?"

"If you're just going to be snarky . . ." Porter gets up to leave, purple ankle and all.

"Sorry." I wave for him to sit back down. "My lips are sealed. Tell me more about this Great Leader."

Porter stiffens as something squeaks behind him and then laughs nervously when he realises he's sitting on Remarkable Student Aisha's rubber duck. "I don't have much to tell. All I know is that while my mother may seem to run LOSERS, the Great Leader is the brains behind it. He's the one that organises the monthly gatherings at Kazinsky Electronics."

"What monthly meetings?"

"When we all gather outside the Kazinsky Electronics store with our iPods. I'm not sure exactly what happens there, but afterwards it's easier to remember the unit numbers of all the portaloos I've seen."

"They must be storing a stronger brain ray in the store. Maybe the one here is just a tester."

"Brain ray?"

"The machine I told you about. The one behind the spy-room mirror," I explain. "The one that makes some people cleverer and some 'not so much'. I think the iPods strengthen its effect."

Porter crushes the rubber duck in his fist until it gives a dying squeak.

"The iPods are evil," he says.

"I don't know about evil, but I do think they're relay transmitters for the brain ray."

"No idea what you're talking about," Porter says, "So I'll stick with evil. You say they've got one of these brain rays at Kazinsky Electronics?"

"I think so."

Porter releases the rubber duck, which gives a wheeeeeeeee of protest. "And the iPods only work near this brain ray thing?"

"That's the part I don't understand," I admit, snatching the rubber duck. "Why bother giving

169

Mum an iPod if there's no chance of her visiting the Mental Conditioning Room or Kazinsky Electronics? They'd need some kind of mobile unit."

Hypatia! I've been blind.

"The Kazinsky Electronics van!" I squeal. "It's a mobile brain ray transporter. That's why it's always parked outside my house. It's zapping Mum."

"Making her smarter?"

"No." That's the hole in my theory. "Exactly the opposite. Since that van appeared outside our house, she's lost interest in everything and just lies there listening to her earphones. My aunt says it's depression, but I'm convinced it's something more."

Porter's hands shake as he rams his memory stick into the laptop. "Sounds like someone I know."

"Gemma Gold?" I ask, handing him the sketch that fluttered from behind my chest of drawers earlier.

Porter rubs at his eyes. *Archimedes!* Don't tell me he's going to cry!

I thrust the rubber duck at him is a desperate attempt to cheer him up. "Here. Have this back."

"Thanks." He grins weakly. "You'd like Gemma. She's great. Smart, like all you geeky types, but sweet too. She even likes talking about portaloos."

I doubt that's true. But I don't want to upset Porter, so I keep my thoughts to myself.

Porter slams the duck against the side of the bath. "After twenty minutes in Mother's Mental Conditioning Room she was like a zombie."

CLUE 34

In at least two cases, the brain ray has had a negative impact on intelligence levels.

I picture the +/- dial.

"They had to send her home," Porter continues. "And I can't get hold of her. Especially not now Mother's got my phone."

"That's why you're keeping secrets from Ms Grimm?"

Porter nods. "She wouldn't help me, so I emailed the Great Leader. He said he'd find Gemma if I did one thing . . ."

"Bring me here!" I finally understand why Porter lied. "But why? What does he want from me? Is he planning to torture me to make Dad do what he wants?" My hands go clammy. "I don't think I'd be good under torture."

Porter's yawn suggests he's less concerned about this than I am. "Can we sort this out tomorrow?" he asks. "I'm exhausted, my foot's killing me and I need to throw myself down the stairs to explain how I got this injury."

"Huh?"

He hops off without explaining. Two minutes lately I hear a loud crash and Porter yelling, "Argh! My ankle! My ankle!"

As I climb back into bed, to dream of kidnap, torture and daft boys who go to ridiculous extremes to explain a sore ankle, I hear Porter groaning in the background.

27

Police

"Mother wants to speak to you after breakfast," Porter says through a mouthful of herrings. "She knows something's up, but she's not sure what."

"Great."

"You might want to ... er ... brush your hair or something."

"Hey!" I protest, but the upside-down reflection in my spoon tells me Porter has a point. I look a state after my sleepless night.

I run back to the dormitory. The hairs stiffen on my arms when I enter my cubicle. Someone installed new locks at the window while I was at breakfast. That must be why I've been summoned.

I shuffle towards Ms Grimm's office, feeling itchy and uncomfortable.

She attacks the minute I enter. "Hawkins. Why were you snooping in my CCTV room?"

Whoa! What? I was expecting to be yelled at about the window.

"CCTV room?" I echo stupidly, wondering whether to deny it or not.

"Don't bother denying it."

That helps.

"I have CCTV footage of the CCTV footage." Ms Grimm presses a button on her desk and a computer monitor rises in front of us, showing images from the CCTV room as well as footage from the screens themselves.

Pythagoras! She doesn't need Jangly Keys Dave's highlights reel. It's all here.

"All very Batman," I mutter.

"Thank you." She gives an outward bow. "So? Are you going to answer my question?"

"Can I ask *you* something first?" I decide to ask her outright if she's kidnapped my dad. I can do this. I take a deep breath.

Ms Grimm holds up a silencing hand as the Bat Screen shows two policemen entering Reception.

The taller officer looks like he's come straight from Holly's favourite American cop show – big and muscular, with a shirt several sizes too small and an abnormally square face. The other man is older with

174

grey hair and twinkly eyes. All they have in common is the walk. They must teach that walk at police school – back straight, head high, eyes scanning the surroundings for trouble.

Ms Grimm dashes from the room and appears a minute later on the Bat Screen, sweaty and out of breath. The policemen stop, abruptly, when faced with that toothy smile, but they're hardened professionals and they don't flinch.

"Afternoon, ma'am," Manly Officer says. "We have received a complaint that your establishment is holding a young female against her will and preventing her making contact with her family."

Ms Grimm's smile looks pained. "I'm sure this is a simple misunderstanding. We do ask our students to hand over their mobiles on arrival, but only because we don't want them distracted during their studies. You know how young people can be."

Manly Officer nods and burbles something about a teenage daughter.

Grey-Haired Officer steps forward. "So students *are* permitted to contact their families?"

I know that voice. It's PC Eric! I should have realised – he looks exactly as I imagined. Red-cheeked and chubby, with kind eyes and big hands, like a clean-shaven Santa.

"We encourage our students to call home every night," Ms Grimm says. "Don't forget these are teenagers, officers. They probably don't speak to their parents that often when they're at home."

It's a good line. Manly Officer smiles in agreement and launches into another complaint about his daughter.

PC Eric doesn't smile. "This girl is close to her parents and they haven't heard from her since early last week. They claim they've been trying to contact her for days and they want to file a missing person's report. I'm sure that won't be necessary if we could just see the young lady in question? Miss Gold?" He checks his notebook. "Miss Gemma Gold."

Ms Grimm pales. Given that she's already the colour of the undead, it's not a pretty sight.

I search the Bat Screen for student registers. "Where are you, Gemma Gold?" I mutter. "Porter thinks you went home, but you obviously didn't. So where *did* you go?"

On screen, Ms Grimm is squirming like an over-sized maggot. "Gemma *is* a student here, but she's away on a field trip. Why don't I ask her to call home the minute she gets back?"

"Perfect." Manly Officer is already at the front door.

PC Eric moves more slowly. "We'll be speaking with the Golds later to make sure they're satisfied. Then we'll arrange a follow-up visit."

"A follow-up visit?" Ms Grimm mutters. "How delightful."

I can't find Gemma's records in the files. *Pythagoras!* Where are they? Ms Grimm will be back any minute. Ah! Here we go.

Click.

I stare at Gemma Gold's photograph. I've been so stupid. Porter's going to kill me.

CLUE 35

The fuzzy-haired girl in pyjamas who I nearly knocked over during my punishment-stair-run was Porter's friend, and missing LOSERS student, Gemma Gold.

28

Locked Doors

I sprint from Ms Grimm's office to the dining room, where I tell Porter everything I've learnt.

He rolls up his sleeves and grabs my hand. "To the rescue!"

"Er, don't we need a plan?"

"This is the plan. To the rescue!"

He hops along the corridors and takes the stairs two at a time, leaving me scrambling to catch up. As we reach the top, I point to the room where I last saw Gemma. Porter bends so his mouth is next to the keyhole.

"Gemma? Are you in there?"

Nothing.

Porter presses his ear to the door. "I swear I heard something."

"Probably the nurse picking up a baseball bat."

"Gemma?" Porter calls, louder now. "It's me. Porter."

"Porter?" The voice is soft and shaky, but this time I hear it too.

"Gemma!" Porter rests his head against the door. "Are you okay?"

"Porter? 'sit reeeeally you?" Gemma slurs. "Wheresssnurse? Whysssohard tuheeeearyou? Why sssuvoicekeepsayindusamefing?"

"Are you listening to your iPod, Gemma? Is that why you can't hear me? Turn it off. Open the door and let us in."

"Cantopendoor. Sssslocked. Voicesssaysssstayin duroom."

Porter stamps in frustration and yelps in pain as he hits his bad ankle.

"Gemma?" I crouch beside Porter and talk, loudly, into the keyhole. "I'm Porter's friend, Noelle. Can I ask you something? Are you wearing turquoise earphones?"

"Yesss. Howdyooknow? WasssmatterwiPorter?"

"Porter's fine," I say, shushing Porter, who's hopping around behind me. "Can you take off the earphones and slide them under the door for us, please, Gemma?"

"Yesss." Gemma's voice quivers. "Icandothat."

Two turquoise earpieces appear beneath the door,

179

followed by an equally turquoise iPod. Porter and I grab an earphone each. Ms Grimm's voice booms through them:

You will stay in this room until I come for you. Then you will ring your mother and tell her you're very happy here. So happy you forgot to phone. So happy you can't talk for long because all your friends are waiting. <crackle> You will forget my son. I have big plans for him. You will not interfere . . .

CLUE 36

Ms Grimm thinks she can brainwash
people into doing what she wants.

Porter yanks his earphone out, pulling mine with it. I'm glad of the relief. A dull pain is spreading through my brain, and after listening for only a couple of seconds, I feel miserable and sluggish.

I remember the mysterious +/- dial on the brain ray.

"Can you create negative brainwaves?" I wonder. "Is that possible?"

Porter shrugs, rubbing his head.

"Even if it is possible," I continue, "why would you bother?"

"*'You will forget my son,'*" Porter echoes.

"You think your mother is stupidifying Gemma so she can keep you for herself?" I force a laugh.

Porter doesn't answer.

"Then why is she stupidifying Mum?" I imagine possible scenarios. "Dad must be locked away like Gemma. She's hurting Mum to make Dad do what she wants. I know she is? *Aryabhatta!* We have to save my parents and destroy Mum's earphones."

"We will," Porter says. "But we're here now so let's release Gemma first."

"We need Jangly Keys Dave to unlock that door."

"Not an option. My mother found out he'd been helping us and transferred him to the kitchen."

Perhaps I don't look horrified enough because Porter adds, "To the fish station!"

"Isaac Newton! Poor Dave."

"Poor *Gemma,*" Porter reminds me. "We have to get her out of there. I wish I knew how to pick a lock."

"I might," I tell him. "I googled it once when I was figuring out the solution to a Tintin mystery."

"Huh?"

"I couldn't work out how the thieves removed King Ottokar's sceptre from a locked room. Turned out it was all to do with cannons and cameras. The locked door was a red herring."

"Rewind to the bit about picking locks."

"I don't know, Porter. It's a bit illegal. What if someone sees us?"

"Kidnapping teenage girls isn't exactly legal either. I doubt Mother will file a complaint. Besides, I don't think this room's covered by CCTV. Locking up students isn't something you want caught on camera."

A logical argument. I like those.

I take Porter through the lock-picking page in my brain, step by step. The only tricky instruction is "purchase a tension wrench and a pick". Fortunately I'm still carrying my mini Meccano screwdriver, and my hairgrip should work as a pick.

It takes a while, but the door finally creaks open.

Gemma is crouched against the wall, hugging her knees, her hair even crazier than I remember. Her eyes are red and swollen, and at the sight of us they widen in panic. Dirt covers her face, except for a few pale streaks where tears have washed the filth away, and she has dried blood around the bottom of her nose. *Another* nosebleed? First Mum, then the student during the maths test, then Aisha and the other Remarkable Student in Reading Hour . . . and now Gemma.

Porter crushes Gemma's iPod beneath his foot. I stare at the remains.

"Gemma?" I grab her by the arms. "This is important. I need you to think. Did you ever have nosebleeds before you came to LOSERS?"

Gemma shakes her head. A phrase from the online medical journal pushes its way to the front of my mind: *"Nosebleeds can be a side effect of radiation poisoning."*

Did the brain ray do this? What if these nosebleeds are my fault? I have to fix things. The first step is to figure out where they're keeping Dad so I can stop them torturing our design secrets out of him.

"What are we going to do with Gemma?" Porter's perfectly symmetrical face droops when he looks at his friend. "We can't send her out alone, not in this state. And with my ankle like this, I'll be no use to her."

"I need to get out of this place to rescue Mum." I glance around frantically. "I'll take Gemma with me. I just have to figure out an escape route."

Easier to say than to do. I walk the whole of the ground floor, but every street-facing window is locked and all the doors are guarded by LOSERS minions.

"There's no way out," I report back to Porter, who's still hiding in the upstairs room with Gemma. "At least not tonight and not without help. Is there anyone on the outside you can call on?"

Porter shakes his head. "You?"

"Not if we don't have a phone. Holly's unreachable now Fake Insurance Man has stolen the computers." I consider Meccano Morris, but his strengths are limited to Meccano-related activities.

"We'll email the police," I decide. "But where can we hide Gemma until they arrive? Someone will check on her soon and then what happens? Maybe the Great Leader could help? The police might pay more attention to an adult."

"No." Porter pulls Gemma towards him. "He didn't keep his side of the deal. We found Gemma on our own. I don't think we can trust him."

I scratch my chin. "I don't think we have much choice."

"Okay. I'll take Gemma to the Great Leader," Porter says grumpily. "But I don't like it."

29

It's Starting

Heed this warning:
The Age of Intelligence is dawning.
Be outside Kazinsky Electronics
at nine tomorrow morning.
Lead the way, while others are fawning.

Porter wakes me at three in the morning by thrusting his laptop in my face to show me the latest group email.

"Fawning?" I mumble sleepily, reaching for the light. "Doesn't that mean giving birth to baby deer? Why would people be doing that?"

"Wake up! And don't turn on the light, you muppet. Fawning also means grovelling. It's a stupid word they chose because it rhymes with dawning. It's not important. What's important is stopping this Age of Intelligence. It can't be a good thing if it leaves people in the state Gemma's in."

"Mmm," I murmur, remembering where we are as my brain kicks into action. "Back here again? Do you have a thing for girls' dorms, Porter?"

"Ugh. Seriously? Imagine if they all wake up." Porter shudders. "Bathroom. Quick."

As my brain moves up another gear, I remember my dream.

Meccano. Eureka!

"Porter, I've got it! We need a Faraday cage!"

"Whatever. Move faster. I need to show you these." Porter reaches into his back pocket and pulls out a pile of Kazinsky Electronics flyers:

KAZINSKY ELECTRONICS:
FREE iPOD GIVEAWAY
Be outside the store at 9 a.m.,
Friday 22nd February

"The 22nd of February? That's tomorrow!" I look at my watch and squeak in horror. "No, it's today! This is happening in six hours' time! You know what an iPod giveaway means?"

If LOSERS give away iPods, they can use
the brain ray on a massive audience.

Porter nods. "It means the Age of Intelligence is about frazzling as many brains as possible. We have to stop them."

"That's why we need a Faraday cage. It'll block the electromagnetic waves."

"English, please," Porter grumbles. "I don't speak geek."

"A Faraday cage is a metal cage built to stop electromagnetic radiation travelling through it. Faraday cages are usually created to shield the things inside – keeping electronic equipment safe from lightning strikes, for example – but we can make a back-to-front version, like a microwave oven, to stop the waves from the brain ray escaping. It'll work as long as the metal is thick enough and the holes are smaller than the wavelength of the radiation."

"Which means . . . ?"

"The maths is a bit boring, but generally a gap of one twentieth of the wavelength will reduce the signal by two-thirds and a gap of one two-hundredth

187

of the wavelength will reduce it by ninety-nine per cent."

Porter's eyes glaze over.

"Meccano and silver foil should do it," I finish quickly. "I need to speak to Meccano Morris. He's always wanted to cover a building with Meccano. This is his chance."

Porter reaches into his pocket and pulls out his phone.

My mouth falls open. "Isn't that supposed to be confiscated?"

Porter waves the hairgrip and screwdriver in the air triumphantly. "I used my new trick! You said we needed a phone, so I took mine. Go on, call your friend."

Meccano Morris is a bit dopey at first, probably because it's three a.m., but he's quick to grasp what I want and says he'll get his brother to fill his van with Meccano and drive over to Kazinsky Electronics.

"We're running out of time," I tell Porter. "We need to get the police involved. They could raid the store and find a brain ray."

"You've got the phone. Call them. Don't forget to mention Gemma. I know we've put our faith in the Great Leader, but how can you trust a man who refuses to show his face."

"You didn't see him when you took Gemma up there earlier?" I ask.

"No. Never have," Porter says. "Isn't that weird? Why would someone want to stay hidden?"

"To avoid being identified as a kidnapper and a torturer?" Another possibility lingers on the outskirts of my brain, but I refuse to let it in.

I hit the phone keys faster.

Policeman: Lindon Police.

Me: **Hello? This is Noelle Hawkins.**

Policeman: [*groans*]

Me: **Are you hurt?**

Policeman: Not physically, no. What can we do for you today, Miss Hawkins?

Me: **I have important news concerning The Case of the Exploding Loo.**

Policeman: At three o'clock in the morning?

Me: **Yes. My dad's alive and has been kidnapped by LOSERS.**

Policeman: Your dad's been attacked by losers?

Me: **Don't laugh. This isn't a joke. You**

189

have to save him. Gemma too, or they'll make her listen to the iPod again.

Policeman: Miss Hawkins, are you aware that wasting police time is a criminal offence?

Me: I'm not wasting time. You are, by not listening to me. You have to find out what's in Mr Kazinsky's Electronics shop.

Policeman: Let me guess – electronics?

Me: That's what they want you to think. But they've hidden a real-life version of my imaginary brain ray in there. I'm worried it'll give people radiation nosebleeds.

Policeman: Let me get this straight. You want us to contact this Mr Kazinsky and ask him about an imaginary machine that makes people's noses bleed?

Me: No! Don't be stupid. If you contact him he'll know you're after him. You need a search warrant. Last

**time I watched *Lewis* I saw . . .
Hello . . . ? Don't hang up. Hello . . . ?
Hello?**

Porter throws a bar of soap at me.

"What?" I protest. "Okay, that didn't go exactly as planned, but the police might follow up."

Porter throws more soap.

"Ugh. Stop it. I swallowed that bit. Look, I'll write a note for Jangly Keys Dave to take to PC Eric. PC Eric will help us. I know he will."

I find a pencil in my dressing-gown pocket and grab a sheet of toilet paper. But it's hard to explain everything – harder still when the toilet paper keeps ripping.

KNOCK, KNOCK.

"Hawkins? I know you're in there? Who are you talking to?"

Fibonacci!

I gaze at Porter in horror. "It's your mother!"

30

Enemies

I glance around the bathroom for a place to hide the phone, the flyers and Porter. Ms Grimm can't know for certain who freed Gemma, but if she finds us plotting in the girls' bathroom, stolen phone in hand, it's not going to look good.

Fermat! There's nowhere to hide. My eyes are drawn to the tiny toilet window. Porter groans when he sees the direction of my gaze. We checked out the bathroom windows earlier as they're the only ones that aren't locked shut, but we decided no one could ever fit through them. Unfortunately, I can't see any other option.

Porter props the window open, glancing miserably at his bandaged ankle.

I jam my loo roll letter into his back pocket, grab

his good foot and launch him at the tiny gap.

"Go straight to the police," I urge him. "Find PC Eric."

Ms Grimm pumps the door handle. "Hawkins? I know you're in there. Open up."

Porter grabs the frame and pulls himself higher. He starts wriggling, yelping as his bum gets wedged in the frame. I push, he pulls. Both of us are sweating with the combination of fear and effort.

Crash!

Ms Grimm keeps coming. She must have unbelievable shoulder muscles.

Smash!

She's almost in.

"Open this door now!" she roars. "Or I will be forced to break it down."

I press my back against Porter's foot to give him something to push against. "Just . . . a . . . minute," I grunt.

"Just nothing. Open up. What are you doing in there?"

"Er. Toilet things. Nearly done." I give Porter a final shove.

"What's that noise? I warned you – I'm coming in."

The wooden door frame splinters under the power of Ms Grimm's assault. We only have seconds and Porter's feet are still sticking out the window. I push with all my strength.

Whoosh!

Whomp!

"Arrrggghhh."

The clatter of the door masks the thump of Porter's crash-landing, but his squeal of pain is unmistakable.

"Arrrggghhh," I howl in an attempt to disguise the sound.

Ms Grimm stares at me.

I rub my stomach. "Must be the herrings."

Ms Grimm pushes past me and searches the bathroom, frowning when it becomes obvious we're alone. "Enough of this foolishness. Get back into bed."

She taps her foot to hurry me along. Maybe it's my imagination, but it sounds like she's beating out the theme tune from *Jaws*.

Everyone else in the dormitory is either asleep or pretending to be. I kick Porter's laptop further under the bed and climb beneath the duvet. Ms Grimm stands over me and glares me to sleep.

I feel like I only closed my eyes a second ago, but the clock reads 05:41. I've been out for over two hours. *Galileo!* How could I have fallen asleep when there's so much to do? I glance around the dormitory. When I'm satisfied Ms Grimm's gone, I root around under the bed for Porter's laptop and find another email. This one's not from your_great_leader@yahoo.com. It's from LOSERS@hotmail.com:

> *The Age of Intelligence will not be defeated.*
> *Our enemies must from victory be cheated.*
> *Ensure they're at this address,*
> *with iPods, at nine a.m.*
> *And your problems will be deleted.*

What does the second line mean? Why does LOSERS'
poetry always sound like it was written by Yoda
from *Star Wars*?

I scroll down to look at the address where everyone is supposed to meet. I'm deafened by the sound
of blood pumping through my body.

It's my address!

CLUE 38

My home is being treated as enemy territory.

Why are LOSERS sending their enemies to my
house? And what does it mean when it says, "problems will be deleted"? Is Mum a problem? Holly? I
have to warn them. But how?

There's only one thing for it. If Porter can squeeze
through that bathroom window then so can I. I dart
into my cubicle and pull on jeans and a thick jumper.
Grabbing my purse, I empty the contents on the
bed. Five pounds and forty-two pence. That won't
get me far in a taxi.

"Are you and Porter helping Gemma?" a voice
whispers in the darkness.

"We're trying to," I whisper back. "But I've run
out of money."

Remarkable Student Aisha slides out of bed. A

minute later she's pressing five ten-pound notes into my hand.

"That's not what I meant," I protest, trying to give it back. "I wasn't asking for a handout."

"Please," Aisha squeezes my hand into a fist, trapping the money inside. "I've been a coward and I'm ashamed. Giving you my birthday money will help me as much as it will help Gemma."

I don't know what to say. There's no denying I could do with the cash.

"Thanks," I murmur.

"If there's anything else I can do?"

"How good are you at pushing people through small spaces?"

31

Rescue Attempt

The taxi driver lets me borrow his mobile to ring Porter. No one has ever sounded so happy to hear from me. I knew Porter was in his pyjamas with no coat when I shoved him out the window, but it hadn't occurred to me that he didn't have any money either.

"A drunk homeless guy felt sorry for me and gave me his blanket. Which was nice," Porter says. "But now I smell like an abandoned portaloo. An early-morning delivery driver offered to give me a lift in the back of his van on condition I held on to his watermelons and stopped them rolling about. But the smell made him retch, so he dumped me at Asda on the outskirts of Butt's Hill. I don't know how to get to the police station from here. I don't know how to get *anywhere* from here."

"Stay where you are. I'm on my way."

The cabbie agrees to pick Porter up but demands an extra five pounds to cover the cost of fumigating his seats. Fifteen minutes later, we arrive at my house.

Porter and I skulk in the back garden and throw stones at Holly's window. I check my watch. 06:42. Holly's going to love this.

After the third handful of stones, she appears at the window, all wide eyes and unruly ringlets. When she sees Porter, she vanishes for a minute and then reappears with a large glass of water, which she pours over his head.

Porter shakes the water from his hair, his breath hanging in the early-morning air as he yells in frustration. "What's next? Burning oil? We've come to rescue you, you lunatic."

"He's with me," I step out from under the tree and wave at Holly.

She grins. "Hey, Know-All. Are you coming up the usual way?" She opens the window wider.

"Can't." I point at Porter's leg. "Window-related injury."

"I'll get the front door," Holly offers. "I haven't heard The Voice for a while so hopefully no one's watching."

I spare a sympathetic thought for poor Jangly

Keys Dave at his fish station and cross my fingers that Ms Grimm is still asleep.

My stomach heaves as we enter the living room. The combination of Porter's blanket and Mum's leftover curry is overpowering. The room looks and smells like a pig sty – or like a pig sty would look and smell if pigs dined on Indian takeaways. Mummy Pig is snoring beneath stuffed Santas and Curry in a Hurry containers, earphones in place.

Porter pretends not to notice and hops towards the small space between the sofa and the window. He beckons for us to follow. Smart thinking. No cameras there and the microphones will struggle to pick up sound. I just hope it's not too late. Mentally preparing myself for a deafening scream, I reach over the back of the sofa and carefully remove Mum's earphones. She grunts, but continues sleeping. *Thank Fibonacci*! I pass an earphone to Porter.

> Rule One: Hang the surrealist picture above the fireplace where Know-All can see it. Never remove it.
> Rule Two: Don't listen to your idiot sister. Listen only to this iPod.
> Rule Three: Stop obsessing about your appearance. You'll give people

the wrong impression. Take that
milkman fellow—

It's the same mechanised voice from the talking shoes.

CLUE 39
The distorted voice on Mum's
iPod sounds familiar.

Before I have time to process what I've heard, I'm
distracted by a movement in the garden. *Tim Berners-
Lee!* Someone must have seen us and called the
troops – Fake Insurance Man, Ug and Thug are
edging along the front path towards the house.

Wallop! Ug batters down the front door.

Crunch! Thug smashes through the living
room, thrusting furniture aside as he heads for
the sofa.

Holly and I pull Porter to his feet – well, foot –
and we stumble across the room in a five-legged
panic, keeping the tinsel-covered coffee table
between ourselves and our attackers and leaving
Mum to sleep through the invasion.

With a savage grunt, Thug swings an ape-like
arm across the table. His fat fist brushes close to
Holly's cheek. She ducks, twirls, seizes one of the

Indian takeaway cartons and throws leftover pilau rice in his eyes. Holly whispers something in Porter's ear and he grabs a handful of broken poppadoms to use as cover fire while Holly slides across the coffee table and drops a carton of chopped red chillies down Thug's trousers.

Thug goes down.

As Holly races towards the front window, Ug powers after her, his boots battering the floorboards while Porter and I pelt him with poppadoms. When he sees Holly reaching for the window lock, Ug throws himself across the room in an attempt to get there first.

Holly hits the floor.

Ug sails over her head and crashes through the window onto the front lawn, leaving a large, hench-man-sized hole in the splintered glass, neatly framed by Christmas lights and fake snow.

Holly jams a sofa cushion over the sharp edges and flings herself out of the house, using Ug's crumpled body as a springboard to jump, run, leap, turn . . . and then stop.

When we reach the window, she mouths "NOW!" at Porter before launching into a sprint. She only manages a few steps before she comes crashing down. I'd swear she paused before diving to the ground and when Fake Insurance Man bundles her into the van she wails in a way that's completely out of character. The Holly I know would be kicking, biting and clawing his eyes out. I swivel to ask Porter what he thinks, but he's fiddling with his phone.

Ug clambers to his feet and Porter raises his hands in surrender, giving me a sharp nudge with his elbow, which I take to mean I should do the same. I lift my arms, happy that surrender now feels strategic rather than cowardly.

Fake Insurance Man stares at Mum, who's still sleep-dribbling on the sofa, and jabs at the screen of his mobile phone. After a brief conversation, he shoves Porter and me towards the van and leaves

Mum where she is. The person on the other end of the phone obviously doesn't consider her a threat; nor do they consider her worth saving from the negative brain ray.

We're halfway down the front path when Mum stirs. She gazes around the room in confusion – it must be odd to wake up without earphones for the first time in weeks. As Porter and I are pushed towards the van, Mum picks up a photo of me from the table by the sofa and hugs it to her chest. I sniff. Must be allergic to something in the van.

"Wait!" I protest. "I want to talk to Mum."

Fake Insurance Man doesn't wait. But just before he bundles us into the van with Holly, I'm convinced I see Mum roll off the sofa and grab the loo roll letter Porter dropped earlier.

32

The Great Leader

When the van stops outside LOSERS, I shove Ug and Thug out the way and storm towards the building. The Grimm Reaper is waiting by the door, perfectly positioned to rip me into bite-sized pieces, but I'm too angry to be scared.

"I want my audience with the Great Leader. And I want it now!"

"I was about to suggest the same thing," Ms Grimm says, which is annoying because it leaves me with nothing to shout about.

As we travel through the turquoise maze of corridors, Ms Grimm confuses me further with niceness and reminds me how well she's treated me since my arrival. Apparently this is the kind of thing I should mention during my audience with the Great Leader.

Her fidgeting is contagious.

As we enter the Great Office, I smooth my hair and fiddle with the buttons on my top. This is more than nerves about meeting someone new. My brain is still in hyperactive shock mode and clues dance in front of my eyes:

(RECAP)
CLUE 7
Someone wants Dad's belongings:
cufflinks, underpants and all.

(RECAP)
CLUE 11
Dad came out of the portaloo!

(RECAP)
CLUE 18
The missing word on Dad's
painting is LOSERS –
the name of Ms Grimm's school for the gifted.

(RECAP)
CLUE 27
Ms Grimm knows Dad and is clearly a fan.

(RECAP)
CLUE 39
The distorted voice on Mum's
iPod sounds familiar.

Part of me knows who I'm going to find in that room, even before the door swings open.

But it's still a shock to see him there, in the flesh and very much alive.

The Great Leader . . .

My dad!

33

Stage Magician

Dad rises from behind his desk, an impressive vision in black velvet until he spoils the effect by tripping over his robes. On closer inspection, the heavy cloak, strange goatee beard and exaggerated hand movements make him look like an ageing stage magician – the kind who pulls rabbits out of hats and sticks knives in his assistants. I wonder what Dad would call himself if he became a magician.

The Great Hawkini? The Incredible Hawk? The Professor?

"Know-All?"

I can't avoid his eyes forever. Why am I even trying? I've been dreaming of this moment for months and when it comes all I can do is gaze into space and make up magician names.

Breathtaking "Big Brain" Brian? Exploding Toilet Man?

I stare at the floor.

Dad's feet turn in Ms Grimm's direction. "Can I have a moment alone with my daughter?"

Ms Grimm taps her ugly left boot in annoyance, but she does as he asks and leaves – probably to watch us on the Bat Screen.

I still can't look at Dad.

"KNOW-ALL!"

I snap to attention and raise my eyes.

Dad holds his arms out towards me. A hug? He can't seriously expect me to give him a hug?

When it becomes obvious I'm not planning to move, Dad makes a big show of stretching and scratching his nose. He pulls out the chair opposite his desk before taking his own seat.

"It's good to see you, Know-All. It's been too long."

"Whose fault's that?"

I sit, but only because my legs are shaking. I don't know how I'm supposed to react. I've imagined being reunited with Dad every minute of every day since he disappeared. Maybe that's the problem: those long days, those long hours, every single one of those long minutes. Only to discover he's not dead, he doesn't have amnesia, he wasn't kidnapped. He just left, to come here and be the Great Leader.

A million questions tie my tongue in knots. A thousand accusations burn the back of my throat. Where to start?

"I hate fish."

Dad twirls his strange little beard and shrugs apologetically. "Mallory's in charge of menus."

Mallory? Ugh. Dad's on first name terms with Ms Grimm.

"I hate violins."

"Mallory likes her music." Dad pulls at his velvet collar. "I've found it's usually best to let her have her own way."

"Most of all, I hate people who fake explosions so they can abandon their families."

Dad stiffens. I've never spoken to him like this before.

"I didn't abandon you. You were always with me – in here." He pats the place where his heart should be. "My daughter. My greatest hope."

I try to believe him. "So where have you been?"

"Here." Dad waves his hand around his office, taking in the multi-screen computer on the desk, the large chess board beneath the window and the pictures of him winning scientific prizes and awards that cover the walls.

Behind him, through a half-open door, is a

bedroom furnished with the items Fake Insurance Man took from our house.

"I've been working to make the world a better place," Dad says grandly. Then he adds, "Besides, I can't leave. People might recognise me."

"What about *my* world?" I search for a picture of me, Holly or Mum among the images on the wall. Nothing. "You didn't make that better."

"You're approaching this from a very negative angle, Know-All. I thought you'd understand my need to complete my research."

"I think you'll find it was *our* research."

"That's enough." Dad adjusts his robes. "No one challenges the Great Leader – Mallory says it's an important part of the image."

Image? Has Dad gone mad?

"I'm not challenging the Great Leader. I'm talking to my dad who's been missing for over two months. It would be weird if I *didn't* have questions – like why didn't you tell us what you'd planned? Or at least let us know you were alive?"

"I did. I left clue after clue. I've been disappointed by your failure to work them out."

He's disappointed in *me*? Arrrggghhh!

"Did you consider that losing my father in a freak toilet accident might have affected my ability to think clearly?"

"I built that into my calculations and still expected you here before the end of January." Dad reaches for a folder on his desk and scans its contents. "It says here you lost a game of chess on Tuesday."

I shake my head in disbelief. This reunion is not going the way it did in my dreams.

"I let Aisha win because I didn't want her to cry again. Sorry."

"You need to toughen up." Dad drops the folder back on the desk. "I hoped my disappearance would help with that."

I squash the urge to pick up the folder and bash Dad over the head with it.

"I thought your disappearance was about making the world a better place," I tell him. "Now it's about torturing me into becoming a tougher person?"

Dad moves the folder out of reach. "This may be hard to understand now, but when you're older you'll realise this has been a valuable life lesson. I never had to explain myself to you before. You've been spending too much time with your aunt and your sister."

"Again. Whose fault is that?"

Dad shakes his head sorrowfully. "So much negativity."

"Me? What about the negative things you and 'Mallory' have done? Let's start with using my calculations to blow up a portaloo and fake your death."

"I apologise. I should have trusted my own equations."

"The equations aren't the part I have a problem with, Dad! But if we're focusing on calculations, you didn't mention the portaloo had air vents. Without them, the explosion would have been far worse."

"I pointed that out to Mallory." Dad shuffles things around in his drawer. "She said it was ironic, people being saved by the smell of their own—"

"It's not ironic," I interrupt. "It's horrible. Someone could have been killed."

"But they weren't – unless you count the old me."

"Where did all that blood come from, Dad? It had to be yours – the police tested it – but that much blood can't have come from a small cut on your foot."

"I took it with me."

The glass on the portaloo floor.

"Test tubes!" I realise. "You got one of your laboratory minions to take test tubes of your blood and then you left them in the toilet with the explosives to make the blood splatter everywhere."

"Good girl! See? You *can* work things out if you try."

I shake my head. "All this planning, all this risk. Why?"

"All great scientists take risks for their discoveries," Dad says. "Marie Curie died as a result of her long-term exposure to radiation during her research."

"Hardly the same thing, Dad. Marie Curie risked her own life. You're risking other people's."

"No one's life is as important as the opportunities the brain ray has to offer. I'll do whatever it takes to develop my invention."

"It's not YOUR invention though, is it? It's OURS."

"We had taken it as far as we could. Mallory offered me space to work, opportunities for testing and access to great thinkers. All I had to do was cut all ties with my old life. She promised you would be looked after."

"The 'cut all ties' part didn't bother you?"

Dad says nothing, just rubs the half-open desk drawer he's been fiddling with since he sat down.

I reach across and yank the drawer open, annoyed by Dad's constant fidgeting. Open-mouthed, I gaze at the contents – hundreds of photos of me. They're not what I expected to see. I look at Dad.

"Mallory told me to get rid of them," he says. "I couldn't."

I remember Ms Grimm's fluttering eyelashes

when she discussed the Great Leader. I remember her voice on Gemma's iPod declaring, *"You will forget my son . . ."*

Her son.

Her Great Leader.

"She wants you for herself. That's what the 'cut all ties' was about. That's why she hurt Mum and put Holly under house arrest."

"Don't be silly," Dad protests. "She was happy to bring you here. She said I could leave clues as long as she approved them first, and she promised that if you were smart enough to crack the clues then she'd consider you worthy to join LOSERS."

"And if I wasn't?"

"I'd have found a way," Dad says, gathering the photos together. "I got you here, didn't I?"

"What about Mum? What about Holly?"

"Mallory needs to be convinced of their worthiness. But I have plans. That's why I liked this place. It's next to your mother's favourite shoe shop. The one with the Jimmy Shoes."

"Mum doesn't shop any more."

"Your mother doesn't do anything any more. I don't understand what's happened to her. She's supposed to be getting cleverer— Ah." Dad catches himself but it's too late.

So he knows about the mobile brain ray. But not

about the positive/negative dial. Does that make things better? Is trying to make Mum cleverer without asking her permission any better than stupidifying her without her consent?

"I don't get it," Dad says. "Why has she let herself go?"

I pound my fist on Dad's desk, making myself jump. "BECAUSE YOU TOLD HER TO," I yell. "On that stupid iPod. I can't prove it was your voice on that machine, but they were your words. I know they were. You have no right to criticise the way she reacted to your death. Especially when YOU'RE NOT EVEN DEAD!"

I pull my copy of the map from my pocket and bang it down on the desk. "And how did you expect me to find you using this? *Archimedes!* No wonder Ms Grimm agreed to let you leave clues if they're all as ridiculous as this one."

"Everything you needed to know was in my painting," Dad insists. "The oversized brain said I had a cunning plan. The finger on the lips told you this was our secret. The long nose suggested everything was a lie . . ."

"All stupid, confusing clues. I'd never have got here without Porter."

"Yes, the boy was useful. Although it may have been a mistake to involve him. He was far more

216

reliable when he did whatever his mother told him."

Speak of the devil. The Grimm Reaper slams back into the room.

34

Disposable People

Ms Grimm stands me against Dad's office wall, hands behind my back.

When the door opens, I half expect a firing squad, so it's a relief when Mr Kumar walks in, followed by . . . Mr Kumar.

"Twins?"

Dad steps forward and introduces Mr Kumar (maths). "Know-All, you've met Mr Amrit Kumar – one of the most advanced thinkers of his generation. Spoke fluently at six months, a guest student of Oxford University at seven. At ten he was invited to America by NASA where he worked for five years. We met at a meeting of the honorary fellows of the Science Museum in London and exchanged ideas on brain science. I was delighted when he agreed to join us here."

Mr Kumar (Curry in a Hurry) steps forward, looking to Dad for a similar introduction.

"And this is Amrit's brother."

Mr Kumar (Curry in a Hurry) steps back sulkily.

I look from one Mr Kumar to the other. "And you're both part of this crazy brain-ray plan?"

Mr Kumar (maths teacher/ubergenius) shrugs and looks at the floor.

Mr Kumar (Curry in a Hurry) puffs out his chest, clearly proud of his drugged hot chocolate and fake iPod loyalty schemes. "Oh yes, we most certainly are."

"It's not crazy," Dad protests. "It's perfect. The brain ray has the power to make the world a brighter place. Who wants to live in a world where phones are smarter than people?"

"Hear, hear!" Ms Grimm sashays towards Dad. "The Age of Intelligence will be my finest achievement."

Dad backs away with an exaggerated cough.

"*Our* finest achievement." Ms Grimm corrects herself.

A louder cough from Mr Kumar (Curry in a Hurry).

"And the Kumars'," she adds quickly. "The Kumars', the Great Leader's and my finest achievement."

I think I might be sick.

Dad sees my reaction and misunderstands it. "And Know-All's," Dad says with an encouraging smile.

"Ugh! No thanks," I say. "I don't want to be part of your finest achievement. I don't want there to be an achievement at all. I want—"

"Shut up! Shut up! Shut up!" screams Ms Grimm, stamping her feet. "I don't care what you want. You're spoiling everything."

"*Me?*" I squeak. "You're the one who stupidified Mum. And *Pythagoras* knows what you've done to Dad. I don't know why he's calling himself the Great Leader. The Drippy Minion would be appropriate."

"I hardly think that's fair—"

"So where's Gemma then, Dad? You were supposed to look after her and hand her to the police. Tell me you didn't take her straight back to *Mallory*."

"You have to see the bigger picture, Know-All."

"I'll take that as a yes. Where is she, Dad? What have you done with her?"

Dad waves his hand dismissively. "She's fine. Perfectly safe. Stop worrying about the little things, Know-All, and start focusing on what we can do here. We can help people achieve their full potential. We can increase the world's intelligence, city by city."

"Don't get ahead of yourself, Dad. You haven't proved the brain ray increases intelligence yet. Lots of other things might be making the Remarkable Students perform better – the fish, the chess, the hideous turquoise walls, the absence of classmates flushing their heads down the toilet. Anything. Maybe they're just working harder because they're terrified." I stare pointedly at the Grimm Reaper. "Even if the brain ray works the way you think it does, then what about the nosebleeds and the head-aches? And what about the positive/negative dial?"

"The what?"

"Ms Grimm hasn't told you about it, has she? You call yourself the Great Leader but you have no idea what's going on because you're too scared to leave this room. There has been a negative brain ray outside our house, on and off, for months. It's on its way back there now. That's why Mum 'let herself go' as you so nicely put it."

Dad chews his lip and shoots a sideways glance at Ms Grimm.

"So what are you going to do about it, Dad? Let your wonderful *Mallory* continue stupidifying Mum? Who knows what effect it's having on her, or on anyone else close by? What about the neighbours?"

"Never liked the neighbours," Dad mutters.

"We're helping those who matter," Ms Grimm says, pushing me away from Dad and back towards the wall. "The others are irrelevant."

"So who's going to look after all these 'irrelevant' people after you've stupidified them? There can't be that many LOSERS to call on for babysitting duty."

"This is not our only programme," Ms Grimm protests. "We have similar courses running in several major cities. The Peterborough branch is particularly strong."

"POSERS?"

Dad gives a half-snigger and covers his mouth with his hand. Maybe he's not completely lost.

Ms Grimm flaps her arms. "These acronyms have become a distraction. Henceforth, we shall be known as The Elite."

"Not by me," I murmur.

Ms Grimm falls into a glary silence. Dad and the Kumars fall into a fingernail-chewing silence. I fall into a wondering-where-Fake-Insurance-Man-has-taken-Holly-and-Porter silence.

I don't have to wonder for long. The answer arrives with a waft of stinky blanket and a kerfuffle in the doorway. Fake Insurance Man marches Holly and Porter into the room, flanked by Ug and Thu—

No, not Thug. Thug trails behind, hands in his

pants. The chillies are clearly still causing him problems.

"Dad?" Holly runs towards him. "You're alive!"

"Yes, yes," Dad brushes her off. "I'm fine. What are you doing here?"

Holly stiffens and she glares at Dad as if she's imagining him spontaneously combusting, one cell at a time.

"I'm here because your evil henchmen kidnapped me and dragged me here," she answers. "How about you?"

"Come and sit with me, Holly," I tug her arm, trying to distract her.

"Sit with you?" Ms Grimm screeches, blocking our path. "Sit with you? What do you think this is? A flaming coffee morning? No one's sitting with anyone." She pushes Holly on to the sofa. "You stay there and don't move. Porter, you sit here where I can see you, and keep that ankle up. Ewww. What is that smell?"

Porter holds out the blanket and ducks behind it so only I can see him. He mouths, "Gemma?"

I glare pointedly at Dad.

Ms Grimm takes one sniff of the blanket and flings it out of the window. She takes a step towards me and I wonder if she's planning to throw me out too.

"As for you, Hawkins . . ." she begins.

Dad steps forwards. "Know-All will stand by me."

I back away.

Porter and Holly fix me with identical stares. I know what they're thinking: we'll have more chance of stopping this if Dad thinks I'm on his side. I stop retreating. But my legs feel like they're encased in concrete that grows thicker and heavier the closer I get to Not-So-Great Leader (and Even-Worse Dad).

Ms Grimm signals for Ug to switch on the large plasma screen. "Flick to the news. I told our local reporter to be outside Kazinsky Electronics from eight forty-five a.m. for the great iPod giveaway."

"*Your* news reporter?" I ask.

"LOSERS has many friends." Ms Grimm beckons to Dad. "Come, Brian. Watch as our invention is introduced to the world."

Dad rubs his hands together like a child preparing to play with a shiny new toy.

35

Newsflash

08:55. The Breakfast News crew cut straight to their roving reporter outside Kazinsky Electronics. In the background, large crowds are grabbing for their free iPods, while police and store security push them back.

"This is Chris Sims with Breaking News – *Lindon Police have intercepted a sinister plot to interfere with the city's brains by launching a series of electromagnetic waves from a machine in the building behind me . . ."*

"Traitor," Ms Grimm hisses as the reporter waves a piece of toilet paper (Is that my note?) at the camera.

"Police arrived at the site in the early hours of this morning, but they weren't the first on the scene. This young man was already here, surrounding the building with metal bars and aluminium foil . . ."

Ms Grimm's eyes narrow as she recognises Meccano Morris from maths class. She pushes her face into mine, showering me with spit. "Is. That. Child. Building. A. Faraday. Cage?"

"Relax, Mallory." Dad puts a hand on her arm. "Look at the gaps. They're too big."

He's right. I didn't give Morris enough time. The cage might reduce the signal, but without a super-human burst of energy, there's no way Morris can stop the effects of the brain ray in time. I glance at my watch.

08:59.

It feels like the room is holding its breath.

Dad raises his hands to the sky. "Prepare for the Brain Wave!"

Ms Grimm raises her hands towards Dad.

Fake Insurance Man and Ug grip the nearest bit of furniture, while Thug roots around in his underpants for chopped chillies.

Holly, Porter and I stare at each other, our faces pale, as the Kumars begin a countdown:

"Five . . . Four . . . Three . . . Two . . . One . . ."

. . . ?

Nothing.

36

What Was Supposed To Happen?

Ug turns up the volume of the news

"The nine a.m. deadline has passed. I repeat, the nine a.m. deadline has passed. And no one here seems to be showing any ill effects. Scientists are on their way to assess the exact nature of the threat, but let me tell you —"

I never find out what he wanted to tell us because Ms Grimm chooses that moment to explode like a Christmas portaloo, destroying furniture, ripping curtains and savaging Kit Kats.

Wait . . . Kit Kats?! Where are the healthy herrings now? Ms Grimm doesn't even break the Kit Kats into fingers. She just devours them in single blocks. I've never seen anyone do that before. It's disturbing.

Dad drops into a chair that isn't there, collapsing

on the floor and muttering to himself, "All for nothing. It was all for nothing."

Thug adds to the madness by unzipping his trousers and dashing into the corridor screaming "Fire! Fire! My pants are on fire!"

A siren wails outside. The emergency services are here. *Thank Euclid!*

"The police!" Holly high-fives Porter. "We did it."

I'm confused for a moment, but then I remember Holly's fake dive in the garden and Porter fiddling with his phone. "Porter filmed Ug kidnapping you, didn't he?"

Holly nods. "And then we sent the footage to the police, along with LOSERS' address."

"Genius!" I murmur.

Holly smiles smugly. "Yes, I probably am."

The adults are less impressed. The sirens snap Ms Grimm and Dad out of their mini-meltdowns. Dad reaches for the keys on his desk. But I get there first.

"What are these for?" I dangle the keys in front of him. "Some kind of movie-villain-style escape pod?"

"I wouldn't describe Mallory's Honda in precisely those terms. We're ... er ... just nipping out for snacks and drinks. Give me the keys, Know-All."

I refuse. "What if you don't come back? You ran away before."

Ms Grimm makes a move to snatch the keys.

Fake Insurance Man blocks her way. "The brat has a point."

Ms Grimm gives him her best Kit-Kat killing stare, but Fake Insurance Man doesn't budge. Instead, he orders Ug to join him.

The stand-off ends when a loud explosion shakes the room.

"What was that?" Porter hops forward and grabs Ms Grimm by the arms. "I want you to tell me where Gemma is. Now!"

"She's back where she belongs," Ms Grimm snaps. "Back where you meddling children should have left her. You'd think that girl was more important to you than your own mother."

Porter grinds his teeth. "It's bad enough to lock her up. But to abandon her when the building's exploding around us? That's just evil!"

Dad shuffles his feet.

Mr Kumar (maths) looks troubled. "You cannot be saying a child is imprisoned within this building?"

"He's not saying anything." Ms Grimm gives Porter a shake and stomps across the room to fling open Dad's office door.

The corridors are full of Remarkable Students scrabbling for the nearest exit. When they realise the doors and windows are locked and no one intends to open them, they start smashing windows, ramming doors and trampling each other to the ground in their desperation to get out.

Through the commotion, Mr Kazinsky barrels down the corridor, carrying a large box of matches in his teeth and rubbing his blackened hands in glee. The CCTV room explodes behind him in a ball of fire.

"Ka-boom!" Mr Kazinsky announces, looking pleased with himself. "I made a Ka-boom!"

"Ka-boom, indeed!" Ms Grimm carefully removes the matches from Mr Kazinsky's mouth. "A little over the top, perhaps, but since the fire's already burning, we should use it. What that fire needs is food. Files, papers, evidence, anything you can lay your hands on. Feed the fire, people. Feed the fire."

Mr Kazinsky leaps around Dad's office, grabbing papers to burn. Dad, Fake Insurance Man and Ug join the frenzy – their disagreements forgotten in the race to destroy evidence.

In the background I hear banging and splintering as the police try to force their way in and Remarkable Students try to force their way out. I don't realise Mr Kumar (maths) has disappeared until I spot him and Aisha half carrying, half dragging a fuzzy-haired girl along the corridor. Aisha is brandishing a large key chain, and smiling for the first time since I met her.

"It's Gemma," I shout across to Porter. "Aisha and Mr Kumar (maths) have Gemma."

Porter sticks his thumbs up and hobbles across to Gemma, who reaches for him, wrinkling her nose and breathing through her mouth as she pulls him into a hug.

Mr Kumar (maths) unlocks the front doors and helps the Remarkable Students to safety as the police force their way in. Fake Insurance Man and Ug slither out among the students and Mr Kumar (Curry in a Hurry) grabs his brother by the collar and drags him along with the crowd, muttering at him ferociously.

Gemma and Porter take over door duty until a teary-eyed blond couple arrive and scoop Gemma up, kissing her again and again, to the point where I can almost feel the saliva. They bundle her into a nearby estate car and drive away quickly. Gemma presses her face against the window, her eyes fixed on Porter as she disappears into the distance.

Porter's chin wobbles, but when he sees me watching he sticks out his tongue and hops down the corridor to help Jangly Keys Dave and his kitchen army throw giant saucepans of water onto the fire. I admire the effort, but if the heat and the flames haven't already killed the CCTV room laptops, the water will finish them off for sure.

Aisha steps forward to man the doors, helping everyone get out and explaining the situation to the police. She can't call herself a coward now.

I rest my hands on Dad's desk, feeling tired.

Pythagoras!

The car keys have disappeared. So have Dad, Ms Grimm and Mr Kazinsky.

37

Kazinsky Electronics

One glance at the plasma screen and I can guess where they've gone. I grab Porter and Holly and drag them out of the school, flagging down a taxi when we reach the kerb. "Kazinsky Electronics. Fast!"

Why isn't the brain ray working? It doesn't make sense. The Meccano cage isn't enough to stop the electromagnetic waves, so what's blocking them?

As we reach the electronics store, the taxi driver swerves to avoid a badly parked turquoise van.

"Those stupid Kazinsky Electronics vans are everywhere," I grumble.

"Dur!" Holly kicks me. "This is the Kazinsky Electronics store. Where else would they be?"

Good point. But they're not all here, are they? One van is outside our house, zapping LOSERS' enemies. Mum!

Mum?

Albert Einstein! That can't be possible!

Behind us in the van we almost hit, her flesh overflowing through the window, is a woman who looks just like Mum. But It can't be, can it? Not Mum who hasn't left the house for months? Not Mum who doesn't even get off the sofa to sleep any more?

I tell the taxi driver to reverse so I can get a better view. It *is* Mum. I'm sure of it! I should have pulled those earphones out weeks ago. Look at her now, out of the house, driving around town in a mobile brain-ray van.

Hang on. *Why* is Mum driving around town in a mobile brain-ray van? The negative brain ray will have no effect if the positive brain ray is switched on. They'll cancel each other out . . .

Eureka!

My skin tingles. "Mum's done it! Mum's created a scalar wave!"

"A scaly what?" Holly clicks open her seat belt as the taxi pulls up to the kerb.

"A scalar wave," I explain. "When two electromagnetic waves of the same frequency meet and are exactly opposite, their amplitudes destroy each other. The energy is transformed back into a *scalar wave.*"

Holly just stares at me.

"Geek speak!" Porter clambers out of the cab, yelping as he puts weight on his bad ankle. "She does it to me all the time. I tell myself it would be worse if I actually understood what she was saying."

"Hey!" I protest. "I am here, you know! I'm saying the combination of the Faraday cage and the negative mobile brain ray that Mum hijacked is cancelling out the super brain ray inside Kazinsky Electronics.

"Mum?" Holly screws up her face. "You're saying Lindon's brains are being saved by Mum?"

I nod. "Before the Curry in a Hurry iPod arrived, I used to sit on the sofa with Mum and talk to her about scalar waves. I had no idea she was actually listening! But she must have picked up the toilet paper note, put two and two together and hijacked the mobile brain ray."

It doesn't sound any more likely when I say it out loud, but maybe that's because I've got too used to thinking of Mum as a zombie.

"I don't see how she could do it." Holly shakes her head. "Not by herself."

"She has size on her side," I say.

"And she's not by herself," Porter adds as the van's passenger door opens and a man wearing a navy sweater emblazoned with the slogan "Milk is not just for kids", clambers out.

"The milkman?" Holly squeaks. "What's he doing here?"

"No idea," Porter says. "But he and your mum appear to have the scaly wave thing covered."

Holly looks at me. "Well, at least one of our parents is on the side of truth and justice," she says. "Speaking of which, where's Dad?"

I point across the road to where Dad, Ms Grimm and Mr Kazinsky are sneaking around the back of Kazinsky Electronics. "They must be on a mission to get the brain ray functioning again."

"Well that's not going to happen." Holly races after them.

Porter and I follow more slowly – Porter because he only has one working leg, me because I'm trying to come up with a plan before I go charging in.

The police have cordoned off the front entrance so we can't get in that way, but Mr Kazinsky has left the back door open (probably for a speedy exit) so we move a few bits of Meccano aside and enter that way, quietly making our way past office rooms and store cupboards full of iPods and other strange looking gadgets.

"Shhh," Holly hisses unnecessarily as we step into the Kazinsky Electronics showroom.

She locks the door behind us and slides the key

underneath it, so we couldn't unlock it even if we wanted to.

"No escape this way." Holly gives a satisfied nod. "Their only chance of freedom now is through the front door where the police are gathered. All we have to do is cover the front exit and yell for backup."

A plan! I like it.

"Where's Dad now?" I ask.

Holly points to PC & VIDEOGAMES where Dad, Ms Grimm and Mr Kazinsky are huddled around a two-metre tall brain ray, that's been set up to look like a game accessory.

"I think they're trying to fix it," Holly murmurs.

"Nothing to fix," I tell her. "It's working. It's just being suppressed by the Meccano cage and then cancelled out by Mum's negative brain ray."

"We need to trap them before *they* realise that." Holly inches towards the TV & HOME CINEMA section at the front of the store. Gesturing for us to follow, she grabs a few boxes from KITCHEN & HOME APPLIANCES and tiptoes towards the entrance.

We are only metres away from the front door when Porter blows our cover.

38

Case Closed

Porter turns to check out a massive plasma TV and yelps in horror as he comes face-to-face with a life-sized cardboard cut-out of Mr Kazinsky. Backing away, he bumps into a shelving unit, dislodging a pile of speakers, which come tumbling down around us.

"Sorry, sorry, sorry," he mumbles, hopping around, stumbling on speakers and knocking into more display shelves. ". . . It's the face . . . ouch . . . sorry, sorry, sorry!"

He's right about the face. Above the cheesy thumbs-up, Mr Kazinsky's cardboard features are locked into a freakish expression of over-excitement. I shudder and give Porter an understanding half-nod. But Holly is less sympathetic. She whacks him with the boxes she took from KITCHEN & HOME

APPLIANCES and then whacks him again as the adults start heading in our direction.

Ada Lovelace! This is a nightmare. Instead of being able to sneakily alert the police, Porter, Holly and I are now in the direct flight path of three deranged adults, all desperate to avoid being caught.

I grab cardboard Mr Kazinsky to use as a weapon. Holly whips two electric kitchen knives out of their boxes and then growls when she realises there's nowhere to plug them in. Porter just stares at his mother and hops back and forth, apologising continuously as Dad, the Grimm Reaper and Mr Kazinsky power towards us.

I manage to slow Mr Kazinsky down by bashing him repeatedly with his cardboard doppelganger and Dad veers off towards the back door when he sees Holly brandishing the kitchen knives. But Ms Grimm continues charging right at us. Despite a heavy barrage by cardboard Mr Kazinsky and several unplugged kitchen knives, Ms Grimm manages to smash her way through both our line and the police cordons and is quickly swallowed up by the crowd.

Holly kicks the wall and then kicks Mr Kazinsky. I edge round her, keeping a safe distance, so I can lock the front door and trap Dad and Mr Kazinsky inside. Porter just stands there, staring at the floor. I remember him stumbling backwards as Ms Grimm approached. Did his ankle give way or did he let her escape? Would I blame him if he did? She's a monster but she is still his mother.

Should I let Dad go free too? I touch the key in my pocket as Holly smacks her palms against the store window to get the police's attention.

"Don't be hasty, Holly." Dad's sweating now. "We don't need to involve the police. You know this was all Mallory's idea."

Porter snorts.

"I had no idea about this negative brain ray," Dad says. "Not until last night."

"That's true." I edge closer to him.

"And what did you do when you found out?" Holly asks.

Good question. I shift back towards Holly.

"I couldn't do anything. Mallory wouldn't let me," Dad says.

"Also true." I don't know which way to move and I need to decide quickly. A group of policemen is heading towards us.

"How did she stop you?" Holly asks. "Did she drug you? Attempt to brainwash you?"

I remember the hot chocolate and the talking shoes. I reach in my pocket and hand the key to Holly.

She takes it and moves closer to the front door. "You must have known something was wrong long before last night," she tells Dad. "You set up the cameras. You could see Mum needed help."

"I'd never hurt your mother. I want to help her. I want us all to be together again." Dad's voice is low with no squeaks.

I try to tell myself he's not lying and he wants to be a family, but Holly's smile makes me nervous.

"Perhaps we can make your wish come true," she says, pointing through the shop window. "Mum's just outside, look! There she is with her scaly wave."

"Her wha—?" Dad's jaw drops open, making it hard to form consonants. "Sca'ar wa—? Noooooo—!"

"I think the milkman helped," Holly adds innocently.

Dad squints through the window and punches a Kazinsky plasma TV, smashing the screen. "Noooooo. Tha' . . . Tha' . . ." Unable to find words to describe the milkman, Dad punches another telly.

"Looking lively for a corpse, Mr Hawkins." Manly Officer from yesterday calls through the glass.

As Holly unlocks the door, Dad stops punching and starts blustering. "He did it," he says, pointing at Mr Kazinsky, who's staring open-mouthed at the broken TV screen. "He's crazy. He started the fire. This is all a terrible misunderstanding."

"Indeed it is," Manly Officer agrees. "You appear to have misunderstood the law and underestimated our intelligence."

I snort and then worry about whether twelve-year-olds can be arrested for disrespecting a police officer. To my relief, a smiling, grey-haired, clean-shaved-Santa figure arrives with a second group of police officers.

"PC Eric!"

He holds out his hand for me to shake. "Noelle Hawkins, I presume!"

Some of his fellow officers groan. Maybe they have food poisoning. I've heard bad things about police canteens. PC Eric frowns at his colleagues.

"It is an honour to meet you in person, young lady. I believe my colleagues owe you an apology."

"That's not necessary." It's easy to be forgiving now I've been proved right. "The police never believed Sherlock Holmes either. Not at first."

One of the younger officers rolls his eyes.

PC Eric stares at him until he mumbles, "Sorry."

PC Eric nods. "Well, they believe you now. You were right about the explosion being faked, right about the shoes being a red herring, right about your father being at LOSERS, right about the need to save Gemma Gold from her iPod, right about Mr

242

Kazinsky's Electronics shop, and right about the imaginary brain ray. Anything I've left out?"

"You listened to my phone call." I smile.

"Of course. I'll always listen to you."

I glance across to where Manly Officer is securing Dad's arms. "Then can I ask you a favour? Will you look out for my dad? I think the brain ray sent him a bit crazy. Maybe it'll wear off."

PC Eric nods. "He will be treated as he deserves."

That doesn't sound good. But Holly's right – Dad had to be stopped.

"There's one final, official duty we'd like you to perform." PC Eric leans forward and whispers in my ear.

"My pleasure," I say, resting my hands on Holly and Porter's shoulders. "I would like to formally declare The Case of the Exploding Loo officially closed."

AFTER THE END

Dad/Great Leader, Wacky Scientist/ Professor Brian "Big Brain" Hawkins . . .

was arrested and remanded in custody. However, because the brain rays mysteriously disappeared and Mr Kazinsky's indoor bonfire destroyed key evidence, there was insufficient proof to charge him with anything connected to his time as Great Leader of LOSERS. Instead, they gave him a two-year sentence for "aggravated criminal damage and endangering life" by blowing up a public portaloo.

I visit him once a week. We're getting on better now I know where he is and what he's doing.

Ms Grimm . . .

disappeared after the police announced they wanted to question her in connection with Gemma Gold's enforced stay at LOSERS, but I don't think she's gone far. Last time I visited Dad, the prison warden said Dad's sister was a regular visitor – which is weird because Dad doesn't have a sister.

He does have a sister-in-law, but Vigil-Aunty says she wouldn't visit him if he was the last man on the planet (which makes sense because Vigil-Aunty has been banned from driving, so if there was no one else left on the planet then there would be no one to drive her to the prison).

When I asked the warden to describe Dad's sister, he said she looked like "Frankenstein's monster after the villagers caught it with their pitchforks." Sounds like the Grimm Reaper.

Holly . . .

won't come with me to visit Dad in prison. She says she's not bitter; she just liked Dad better when she thought he'd spontaneously combusted. In contrast, Holly and Porter are getting on like a house on fire. (Not literally. Setting buildings on fire is illegal as Mr Kazinsky discovered when they locked him up after the explosion.) And with Porter acting as nego-tiator, Holly and I are, well, not exactly friends, but she doesn't kick me as often.

Porter . . .

managed to get through to Gemma by phone. Once. But when her parents discovered he was Ms Grimm's son, they banned all further contact. Mum was so moved by the tale of star-crossed love (and so surprised I'd made a friend) that she invited Porter to move in with us until his mother turns up again. It helped that he offered to pay rent. He can afford it. Following Dad's trial, Porter's Exploding Portaloo movie went viral with over a million hits on YouTube, swelling the number of portaloo spotters from approximately four to tens of thousands.

Mum . . .

left the sofa for several days to help with the police investigation. During this time, she built a huge bonfire in the garden for Dad's picture, the brain-washing iPod and the Curry in a Hurry leaflets (which we no longer need as Curry in a Hurry rapidly relocated, shortly after Dad's arrest). But, after that brief flurry of activity, Mum decided life was far more relaxing when viewed from the sofa and returned to her sedentary lifestyle.

LOSERS ...

shut "for refurbishment" and many parents removed their kids altogether. But some were so impressed with the improvement in their children's test results they re-registered them after Mr Kumar (maths) agreed to act as temporary head.

Me ...

My life is good. Now Dad's a famous "banged-up" criminal, I have even been invited to join the Toilet Trolls. But I don't need new friends. Not when I've got Holly, Porter and Meccano Morris – who has become a bit of a celebrity after helping to save the day with his Faraday cage. Besides, if I had more friends then I wouldn't have time to look for new cases to solve ...

Acknowledgements

With thanks . . .

To my little Know-Alls for making me smile and checking this book contains the right amount of poo – Jodie, Dylan, Hugo, Amber, Sami, Ruby, Oscar, Maisie, India and Kristiaan.

To my big Know-Alls for being wise in the ways of brain rays, police cordons and portable toilets – Cousins Chris & Giles, Eloise and Stuart Payne (who are not related), Adam McCarthy, Matthew Bage, Omar Ismail and his very clever wife who doesn't like to be named.

To my friends who read the book and said nice things about it. That would be you Ellie, Charlie,

Tracy, Alice, Annabel, Maria, Svenja, Sam, Tony, Jack and The Other Rachel.

To teachers everywhere, because people don't thank them enough. But particularly to Emma Hall, Lynne Doyle and Kelly Wass for making a quirky kid proud to be different.

To the Emirates Lit Fest folk, Luigi Bonomi Associates and Montegrappa. Because I like prizes.

And to my mum, my sisters and my husband. For everything.